Southern Fried Son of a Gun

A Willow Crier Cozy Mystery

Book 4

Lilly York

Southern Fried Son of a Gun

A Willow Crier Cozy Mystery

Book 4

©2016 by Lilly York

www.lillyyork.com

Cover Design: Jonna Feavel
40daygraphics.com

Illustrations: Ben Gerhards

Interior Layout: Daniel Mawhinney
40daypublishing.com

Published by: Wide Awake Books
wideawakebooks.com

Also available in eBook publication

Printed in the United States of America

Get your free short story!

Grandpa Goes Missing

Find out what happened to bring Willow down to Oklahoma in the first place.

FREE short story only available here!

www.lillyyork.com/shortstory

Get yours today!

Chapter 1

The heat-seeking missile sat poised, ready to fire. She took aim. The target locked. She fired. The explosion rocked the intersection…

"Mom? Hello, earth to mom."

Willow startled out of her daydream. "What?"

"What were you just doing?"

"Nothing."

"Mom, answer the question."

She pointed to the red pickup truck in front of them. "I just blew him up."

Embry raised her eyebrows. "A little extreme, don't you think?"

"I tried to be nice and let him through. Did he go through? No. He cut."

"He cut? Isn't that a little middle school?"

Willow guffawed. "It's also perimenopausal. Let's not leave that out." She accelerated. "I was in line first. I was being nice and didn't want to block the intersection so I gave him room to pass through. Did he? No. Instead he cut in line. He didn't even acknowledge me. He had to go."

Embry shook her head. "Mom, it was McDonald's drive through. I'm not sure you should have a gun. It might not be the wisest decision."

Willow patted her purse. "Oh, Honey, it's fine. Just because I want to rid the world of all the idiots doesn't mean I will."

Willow pulled into the parking space in front of a rather drab, dirty brown building. "Are you ready?"

Her gun club was meeting for a potluck. The concealed carry class Steve signed her up for got along so well they had decided to get together socially. Willow had decided food was the one way to get Embry to the club.

"Ready as I'll ever be. I guess." Embry opened her door. "Do I have to do this?"

"Yes. You do." She paused. "Well, I guess you don't— but if you ever want me to make homemade chicken potpie again you will."

"Mom, that's not fair."

"I don't play fair. Never claimed to either." Willow led the way to the front door and held it open for her daughter, then followed her in. The entry was a mini store and had glass cases with a few guns and some ammo. "You work downtown, sometimes late at night. I've seen the kind of people who are wandering around at that time of night. I'll feel better knowing you can protect yourself."

A deep southern voice ended their conversation.

"Willow, hey, how you doin', girl?" The elderly man looked to Embry. "Don't tell me. She's your sister, right?"

Willow grinned. "Flattery will get you everywhere. Clancy, this is my daughter, Embry. Embry, meet Clancy." She addressed Embry. "Clancy is a war hero."

"Girl, don't be goin' on about me. She don' wantta be hearin' no old war stories. She got better things to do than that."

Willow frowned. "Clancy, you should be proud of what you did. Not everyone would risk their own safety to help others. Especially if they weren't exactly friendly toward you."

He waved her off. "Nah, anybody would have helped. I'm nothin' special."

He went behind the counter and glanced at his watch. "You're a bit early for the potluck. What can I help you two ladies with today?"

Willow loved Clancy's range. It wasn't fancy like the others in town. It was a little off the beaten path and if you wanted a cup of coffee or a soda, your only choices were the vending machine or the crusty pot Clancy kept on the counter. Granted, the coffee would put hair on your chest but once you got used to it, it was almost like coming home. She smiled. "You got me. My dish is in the cooler in the Jeep. Since I was coming anyway, I thought I'd get some practice time in." She motioned to Embry. "She's never shot a gun. I want her to be able to protect herself. So, I'd like two lanes. And a rental for Embry."

Clancy nodded. "You got it." He pulled out a Smith & Wesson revolver and some ammo. "This should do the trick. Jason, can you give this young lady a rundown on the 1911?"

"Sure Mr. C." Jason put his duster behind the counter. "Which lane did you assign to her?"

"I put 'em in eight and nine. Maybe you can use the classroom and go over the rules and the gun."

Jason nodded, took the gun and the ammo, and walked away.

Embry gave her mom a look then shrugged and followed the young man with the buzz cut through a hallway and into a small classroom. Willow entered right behind them. A refresher course wouldn't hurt, nor would learning about another weapon.

A half hour later, Jason led both women to their lanes and got them each set up with a target. "OK, why don't you give it a go and I'll stay here and help you out for a bit."

Embry loaded the weapon as she had been instructed, then took aim and fired. She looked to Jason for input. He simply nodded so she fired again.

This time he interjected. "You need to keep both eyes open."

She nodded then fired again, making sure both eyes were fully open.

Jason motioned for her to set her weapon down and he brought the target forward. Two shots were on the paper but to the right of the silhouette. One was in the chest. "See what happens when you are aware of your target? You hit it." He sent a clean target out. "Let's try it again."

She spent her round of ammunition and then drew in the target. Every shot was a hit. Not all were kill shots, but she did have a couple. As much as she didn't want to like firing a weapon, she had to admit, it felt good. Jason seemed impressed as well.

"You're good at this. How long have you been target shooting?"

"This is my first time."

"You're kidding? I never would have guessed." After watching her load her weapon, he excused himself. "If you need anything just give me a yell."

Willow watched as Embry put her earplugs in and joined her in warding off various criminals. All put out of their misery, of course. She knew her daughter would be a natural. It would have to run in the family.

Shortly before their time ran out on the lanes, the lights flickered. Willow glanced around, but nothing seemed out of the ordinary so she finished off her round and cleaned her gun as she waited for Embry to do the same.

"Well, what did you think?"

Embry's face lit up. "I loved it. I didn't think I would, but I did."

Willow laughed. "I knew you would."

Together they turned in Embry's weapon to Jason. "Clancy taking a break? He's joining us for the potluck, right?"

"Yeah. He's out back taking a smoke break." He rolled his eyes. "He'll be back in a few minutes."

Willow holstered her gun and went for her cooler. She made a broccoli salad and chocolate chip cookies. She also picked up a couple of gallons of sweet tea.

Birdie pulled into the parking spot next to Willow's Jeep. Willow waved but Birdie didn't appear to see her.

Birdie drank copious amounts of caffeine. She flitted from one thing to another. Willow wasn't sure how it was possible for her to hold a gun still enough to hit any target, let alone one about to cause her physical harm. Willow watched as she popped out of her boxy Scion and started for the building. Suddenly, she turned around.

"Willow, so sorry. Didn't see you there."

She approached Willow and took the two gallons of tea from her, then turned for the building. Willow lifted the cooler and tried to catch up, to no avail, of course. By the time Willow entered the classroom everyone was thanking Birdie for remembering to bring something to drink. The woman continued on as if she didn't hear them. She neither accepted their thanks, nor denied she brought the sweet drink. Willow had gotten used to her demeanor. Classic Birdie. Today, Willow chose to ignore it. She'd already blown up one vehicle and taken out an army of bad guys. The range was great for working off aggression. Birdie was safe—for today.

Willow placed her salad and cookies on the conference table. She noticed Embry was still talking with Jason and wondered what Marshall would think of that. "You two seem to have a lot to talk about."

Embry blushed. "Jason was telling me about Clancy's time in Vietnam."

So maybe everything is all right with Marshall then, good. I really like that young man. "Interesting, huh?"

"I'm not sure interesting is the right word. Makes me want to smack somebody."

Willow laughed. "You better be careful. Next thing you know, you'll be blowing up trucks in intersections." She looked around. "Clancy's been gone a long time. Longer than normal. I wonder if he's OK."

Jason scoped out the room. "I'll go look out front. Maybe he had a customer come in."

More of her classmates filed into the room. Someone made fried chicken. Willow could smell it and looked down at her growling stomach. "Traitor." She had every intention to lose a few pounds. Funny how being in a new relationship did that to a girl.

She selected a breast from the glass pan and added her broccoli salad with a helping of fruit to her plate. She added a small portion of what looked to be homemade macaroni and cheese. The creamy concoction was a downfall of hers. She had many. Her hips didn't lie. She sat down next to

Embry who happened to choose the table Birdie was at then took a bite of the pasta. "Eww…this has olives in it! Who does that?" She grabbed a napkin out of Embry's hand and spit the nasty mixture into it. "Oh, that was terrible. I hate olives."

Birdie exclaimed, "I didn't make it with you in mind! I love olives. I wanted to try something different." She stood up and moved to another table, obviously offended.

Willow looked at Embry. "How was I supposed to know?" She took a bite of her broccoli salad to remove the taste of olives from her mouth. She loathed olives. Just as she picked up her chicken, Jason appeared looking as if he was going to be sick.

"Jason, what's wrong?" Willow scanned the room. "Where's Clancy?"

He nodded, then turned. Willow quickly followed him outside and around the building. She was thankful she hadn't taken a bite. If she had, she would be losing it.

A bare electrical wire, running from the box on the back of the building and partially buried was protruding from the ground in the overgrown weeds. Clancy was unmoving, lying on the ground. Wires just don't all the sudden start popping out of the ground. No way could it have been an accident. The means of death was obvious: someone fried their host.

Clancy Cobb was electrocuted.

Chapter 2

Willow's mouth hung open. The smell wasn't pleasant. Neither was the vision. Some things just can't be unseen.

Willow tried to keep Embry from approaching. She was unsuccessful.

Embry tossed her cookies. Literally. She'd downed several of her mom's homemade chocolate chip cookies and wasn't sure she'd ever be able to eat them again, even if they were the best cookies she'd ever eaten.

Neither Embry, Jason, nor Willow noticed the stranger standing next to the dead body until the police arrived and led them all from the scene. All four of them were waiting to be questioned in the break room. The rest of the party goers were being held in the conference room, with the food. Not that Willow could even think of eating. Well, maybe a little—but just a little, no more.

Pacing around the small table the others were sitting at, Willow finally noticed the tall, well dressed elderly gentleman. She stopped before him. *Where in the world did he come from?*

Never one to mince words she asked, "Who are you?"

He gave her a half smile. "I've never blended in before. Are you just taking notice of me?"

She shrugged her shoulders. "I'm sorry. With everything…"

He extended his hand. "No worries. I understand perfectly. I'm Abel White. Betcha didn't see that comin' now did ya?" He held up his dark ebony hand and laughed at his own joke. "I served with Clancy in the war. We've been friends a long time."

Willow appraised him while slowly nodding. He looked and sounded just like a southern gentleman. She deemed him good people and extended her own pale hand. "I'm Willow. Nice to meet you, Abel. Although it could have been under better circumstances."

"I have to agree with you there. I'll miss the old guy."

"So, what were you doing here?"

For this he grinned. "Clancy invited me. He makes the best fried chicken you ever did taste. I don't know what he does to it, but it sure is good. He could have opened a chicken restaurant and gave the Colonel a run for his money." He rubbed his stomach. "I sure hope there's a piece left. I don't want my last bite to be my last memory."

Embry's mouth hung open. "Did he make the fried chicken for the potluck? I got one bite before I went outside. I thought I'd died and gone to heaven."

"Yep. It'll do that to you."

The door opened and a police officer led a stunning young woman to Abel. "Grandpa, are you OK?"

He pulled her close. "I'm just fine. Don't you worry about me."

"Willow, meet my granddaughter, Jordina. Jordina, this is Willow." He made introductions then quieted down for the police officer.

"Mr. White. The detective is ready for you. Do you want to follow me?"

Jordina gave her grandfather a hug, then sat down at the table and waited. Willow sat down next to her and placed her hand on the young lady's arm. The girl couldn't have been more than 19—20 at the most. She was tall, lithe—definitely model material. "It's going to be OK. This is just procedure. He'll be out in a few minutes." Willow breathed in deeply. Whatever perfume Jordina was wearing was fantastic. Original. She wanted to ask what perfume it was but didn't think this was the appropriate time.

Jordina's brow furrowed. "How can you be so sure?"

"Well, I hate to admit it but I've been through this before. The police always question whoever was around. It's best we tell them everything we noticed—no matter how insignificant it might seem—because this is when we remember the most. And our minds haven't had a chance to change any details on us yet."

Jordina started crying.

"Honey, your grandpa will be out here eating chicken before you know it. Well, if those buzzards in the other room haven't eaten it all."

She wiped her tears and tried to smile. Even in tears she was beautiful.

Willow pulled a tissue out of her purse. "Here you go."

She delicately dabbed the tears without messing up her makeup. She smiled. "Thank you."

"You're welcome. It's all gonna be OK. You'll see."

Her eyes filled with fresh moisture.

"You don't understand. I think my grandpa did it."

Chapter 3

Before Willow could ask why Jordina thought her grandfather killed Clancy, he reappeared and Jordina ran into his embrace. *Guess that'll wait.* The police officer called her name and she looked up, questioningly. "Oh, yeah. Right." She grabbed her purse and followed him into the makeshift interrogation room, Clancy's office.

She sat down where he indicated and she waited. The questioning was really a formality. There was video feed of her and Embry being in the lanes the entire time leading up to the time of the murder. Mainly, the detective just wanted to know if she'd heard or seen anything that might help them find out what happened.

"The only strange thing that happened was when the lights flickered on and off a few minutes before our time on the range ended." She glanced at her watch. "That would have been around 3:45, 3:50."

The detective asked, "Did you see anyone suspicious? Anyone lurking about?"

"Suspicious? No. Lurking? Yes. The maintenance man gives me the creeps. But that doesn't mean he killed Clancy. I just always catch him staring. It's probably nothing."

The police officer jotted down his notes and thanked her. Embry was questioned before Jordina, so she was waiting for Willow in the hallway. Willow pulled her aside. "Let's go back in by the potluck. I want to try and catch up on some gossip." Her stomach growled. "Besides, I'm still hungry."

Little groups of whisperers were standing all around the room. Willow and Embry went straight for the buffet. She was glad to see Abel and Jordina already sitting down eating. He even had a piece of Clancy's chicken.

Willow's former plate disappeared so she made a new one then sat down next to Abel. Embry sat across from her, next to Jordina.

"This is delicious. You're right. Wow. Even after sitting."

Abel wiped his mouth. "Especially after sitting. That's why it does so well in contests. Some chicken goes a little limp. But Clancy's, well, his gets even better tasting. I guess this will have to do me." He took another bite.

The four were quiet, each one busy eating. Being interrogated for a murder made a person hungry. Perhaps it was knowing Clancy would never eat again. Perhaps it was because all four knew they would never again have his chicken. Whatever the reason, all four cleaned their plates.

Willow pushed back first. She noticed even Jordina ate well. She would have guessed the girl ate like a bird as thin as she was. But, she had a healthy appetite. *Must be a high metabolism. What I wouldn't give for one of those!* She wiped her hands on her napkin. She would have loved to get Jordina alone. She wanted to know what the girl meant about her grandfather being guilty. But, an opportunity never arose. Abel stood and after throwing his trash away, he told both Willow and Embry he would see them at the funeral. Jordina kept her eyes downcast as she followed after her grandfather.

After watching them walk through the door, Birdie stepped up beside Willow.

"Did you try a piece of Clancy's chicken? I think it might be the best fried chicken I've ever tasted."

Birdie scrunched her eyebrows. "I've had better."

Chapter 4

"Hey, what happened?"

Willow turned toward the voice that always put a smile on her face no matter what mess she found herself in. "Hi." She leaned forward and allowed herself to be hugged. "Clancy is dead."

Steve pulled back so he could see her expression. "Tell me what happened."

She went through the story again, for Steve's benefit. She talked, he ate while he listened.

"So, I take it his death wasn't natural causes?"

"You'd be guessing correct. He was electrocuted."

He pushed his plate away. "I want to see the crime scene."

She stood up. "Come on, I'll show you."

The area was cordoned off so Steve showed his badge and was allowed in. Willow wasn't given the same respect, which totally drove her crazy. She had to stay behind the yellow tape.

Willow pushed against the tape nearly to the point of snapping. The officer stood in front her, warning her with his eyes. She watched Steve's mouth move. "What did you say?" She yelled to Steve. He said something but she couldn't hear a word of it. She addressed the officer. "Could you go ask him what he said? I can't hear him."

He shook his head in disbelief and walked to the other side of the large circle.

Steve waved her off and continued walking around the site, talking to himself then to the police officer who was making sure the scene remained uncontaminated. Willow had tried to reason with him—she was the one who found the body, well, the second really but she failed to bring up that little bit of information. It didn't matter, she wasn't allowed in regardless.

Willow leaned in again, trying not to get irritated at the obvious lack of respect being shown her. She'd solved three previous murders. Did that not count for anything?" Suddenly the tape snapped and Willow quickly turned her back, hoping the police officer didn't notice it was her doing.

After what seemed like forever, Steve made his way back across the now defunct tape.

"What did you find?"

"There are two sets of footprints. Someone was with him. It had to have been someone he trusted, someone who knew he went out back to smoke."

"That could have been anyone in the building, as well as half the town."

"Well, whoever it was knew enough to plan ahead. The wires had been stripped down, buried with the bare ends exposed, and ready for the murderer to use them whenever he had a chance."

"Or she." Willow corrected.

"Yes, or she. Someone would have to have a fairly good grasp of electricity and how currents work."

"That rules me out. Sometimes I plug my hair dryer in really fast, just in case. Especially when there's a little bit of water on the counter." She shuddered. "What a horrible way to go."

"It wouldn't have been pleasant, that's for sure."

"Doesn't Clancy have surveillance cameras?"

"Just for the inside and the front and side parking lots. Since there isn't a door back here, he wasn't concerned about the back of the building or the other side. I guess he should have been."

"Will the angle of the camera show anyone slipping around the corner?"

"The police have already collected the tapes and are going to go through them. Clancy had a one week loop. If our guy, or gal, prepped a week and a day ago or they knew the camera's blind spots, they won't be on film. But, if the killer actually knew that bit of information, and planned for it, then it's someone familiar with how the range is run."

Willow nodded her head. "Very true. I guess we'll find out soon enough." She followed Steve as he led her back around to the front of the building. Their relationship was easier, less complicated before that kiss. She smiled to herself. *But, that kiss was amazing!*

"What you thinking about?"

Willow's face turned redder than the Oklahoma dirt. "Um, nothing."

"Mom! I've been looking everywhere for you."

Willow could have kissed her daughter. "You were busy talking to Jason. I didn't think you'd notice I was missing."

Embry glanced at her watch. "I've gotta go. With everything going on, I totally spaced out meeting up with Marshall." She smirked. "And since you forced me here, in your car, I have no choice but to have you take me home to get mine." She shrugged in the direction of Steve.

"Hey, why don't you take your mom's Jeep and we'll swing by later to get it." He looked at Willow. "If that's OK with you?"

"Sure. Why not?" She wiped the sweat dripping from her brow. "I don't care as long as I get into some air conditioning, and soon!" She handed Embry her car keys. "Just leave them on your kitchen table." As she watched Embry leave she asked, "When are we going to get some cooler weather?"

"It's only the beginning of September. We won't see cooler temps for at least a month, if not longer."

"Let me get my stuff then we can be off."

Steve helped her carry her dishes and cooler to his truck. "Want to go on a field trip?"

She didn't have to even stop to think. "I'm game. Where to?"

"I never told you how I know Clancy, did I?"

She shook her head.

He smiled. "You're about to find out."

Chapter 5

Steve pulled up in front of a pretty simple looking cabin and turned off the engine. "My family has owned this place for years. We all use it when we have time. It backs up to the lake and reminds us of our childhood. My grandparents bought it when my dad was about 10 years old. We have a pontoon boat and a pier. Makes for some great lazy days."

Willow stepped out of the truck, carefully. She hated snakes. Couldn't stand them. Shortly after moving to her place she had Embry drive her Jeep around the property and she used Gramp's old shotgun and shot anything that looked like it moved. That was the second time she encountered the gentleman sheriff who now held her heart. Turned out the place she inherited was in the city limits. And shooting was pretty much frowned upon. Looked like country to her.

She followed in Steve's footsteps. She had worn tennis shoes. When she traipsed around her own place she took the dog with her and she wore boots— protective boots. She shuddered thinking about the slithering beady-eyed beasts that might be lurking in the overgrown grass she was walking through. "Don't you believe in mowers?"

"Sorry, haven't had time."

"Can you walk any faster?"

Steve shot her a glance over his shoulder. "Are you in a hurry?"

She didn't want to sound like a scared little girl so she thought she'd use the excuse that always worked. "Gotta go, if you know what I mean."

Steve grinned. "Oh, well, then you best head around to the back of the cabin. We never got around to putting in a bathroom. We still use the old outhouse."

Willow stopped in her tracks. "What?"

"Yeah, we wanted to keep the cabin rustic. It reminds us of what our ancestors had to put up with. Gives us perspective."

"I'll hold it."

"Are you sure? It's right around back." He chuckled.

Willow grimaced. These days even the mention of a bathroom made her have to go. *What was I thinking?* "No, it's okay. I'm good."

He unlocked the front door and held it open for her. The inside was of simple construction, but it was absolutely beautiful. A huge stone fireplace filled one wall and there was an up-to-date kitchen, all open living with gleaming wood beams, wood floors, and plank walls. She could hardly believe this place didn't have an inside toilet. "It is a lot bigger than it looks." She eyed him suspiciously. "And not quite as rustic as I was led to believe."

He laughed. "OK. So, it's all up-to-date, including the bathroom." He pointed toward a hallway. In fact, there are two bathrooms. Take your pick. And you won't find a single snake to avoid." He looked out the large glass window into the back yard. "But hurry up. I have something I need to show you."

"Ugh!" She scampered down the hallway and located a bathroom.

A few minutes later, she found Steve in the backyard sitting on a pier and an empty chair next to him obviously intended for her. "You want to show me the lake?"

"As beautiful as it is, no. See the cabin directly across from us?"

She peered across the small lake. "Yes."

"That cabin is where Clancy lived, full time. Not just weekends." He patted the chair. "Sit. It's almost show time. I'll be right back."

Willow sat down as Steve stood. She watched his retreating backside then turned toward the lake.

He returned with tall glasses of iced tea and a package of store bought cookies. "Sorry, I know they're not homemade, but, it's all I've got."

She plopped half a chocolate covered graham cracker in her mouth and mumbled. "My favorite store bought cookies of all time!" A few crumbs fell out and she pushed them back in and grinned.

Steve lifted his binoculars. "Here we go. I was kind of surprised we beat him here. He left a good half hour before we did."

He handed them to her in time for her to see Abel White picking the lock to the Clancy's cabin. "Oh…he had to take his granddaughter home first. But, how did you know he'd show up?"

"Human nature." He lifted his camera with a long lens attached and began taking pictures.

How did I miss that? Had to be when I was watching out for those darn snakes! She started to rise.

"Where are you going? Back to the bathroom?"

"No, I figured you caught the culprit. His own granddaughter thinks he's guilty."

He glanced at her sideways. "We're not done yet. In fact, I'd bet we're far from it."

Her mouth dropped open. "You think there'll be more visitors?"

He nodded and added, "Yep. I'd say several." He lowered his camera as Abel made his way into the house. "Remember, I know this man. I know some of his secrets. He's a good guy, but he hasn't always been. I believe a few people today will be trying to protect their secrets and one will be trying to hide the fact they are a murderer. We must take note of everyone who enters the house. From there, we work out who is who."

Steve looked at his watch. "If he doesn't hurry, there is going to be an overlap."

Willow was incredulous. "Shouldn't you do something about this?"

"Well, I suppose I could. Except I won't. First, I have no jurisdiction. Second, how would we then know who our primary suspects are? Third, I thought you'd enjoy this. And fourth, you don't think I didn't clear this with OKC PD do you? Why do you think they're taking their sweet time showing up to the house?"

She laughed. "I should have known and yes, you're right. I am enjoying this." She lifted the binoculars and scanned the road beyond Clancy's cabin and gasped with her air intake. "I don't believe it. No way."

"What do you see?" Steve reached for the binoculars and she leaned out of his reach.

"It's Birdie. I'm sure that's her Scion. But, what is she doing here?"

"Oh, Abel's gonna be caught red handed if he doesn't get out of there soon."

"Nope. She slowed down but passed the driveway. She must have seen his car."

"I wonder if she knows who the car belongs to."

"I don't think she's gonna have a problem with that. She parked a little ways down and is now on foot. I think she's gonna spy on him. At least that's what I'd do." She looked at Steve. "That woman must be crazy. She's trying to hide behind a tree wearing bright yellow. Who does that?"

He shrugged then attempted to find her through his long range lens. He gave up on getting the binoculars back.

Willow heard the click of his camera. "You found her, then?"

"The yellow in the middle of all that green and brown kind of gave her away. But what is she doing?"

Willow focused back in on Birdie. She was hopping around like a disoriented bunny. Arms were flailing and she was jumping in circles. "I have no idea." She shook her head and continued watching the spectacle.

"She might be on drugs."

She laughed. "You think?" She turned slightly toward the house. "Clancy just hurried out the front door without bothering to lock it. Birdie will be happy, if she even notices him leaving." Willow watched the crazy woman. "She just ran into the lake, clothes and all."

"I'm glad she didn't strip. Goodness. That would have given all the old coots around the lake watching the yellow bunny a show."

"She's done with her afternoon swim, now she's walking toward the house. She went in without bothering to dry off. I guess she doesn't care she's tracking water all over the place."

Steve was clicking away on his camera. "This is better than I thought it would be." He rested his camera, but she exited just a couple of minutes later, obviously in hurry to get out of there so he took a few more shots. Not only that, she didn't cut back through the woods to her car. This time she took the driveway and ran down the road.

"Huh. That is one odd woman."

For the next half hour all was quiet. It seemed as if their afternoon of spying was over when a red sports car pulled in the drive way.

Willow would never have guessed that Jordina would have any reason whatsoever to show up at Clancy's place. "I know she didn't murder him. She's certain her grandfather did."

[33]

Steve quit taking pictures. "And when were you going to tell me this?"

"Oh. I didn't did I? I thought I had." She nodded her head. "I swear I'm going senile. Seriously. I forget everything." She told him what Jordina had said.

"Are you basing your opinion of Ms. Jordina on her performance today at the questioning? Some people are very good actresses. And they are pretty good at playing a part."

"I guess I hadn't thought of that."

Before dark, Clancy's cabin had two more visitors. Jason, Clancy's part-timer, and Garth, the maintenance man. Steve made a quick phone call and let the police know who had been visiting, then he and Willow packed up. He opened the front door and locked it, then scooped her up and carried her to the truck. "You really think I'm going to let you get bit by a snake? Never." He deposited her in the front seat. "Besides, I know the damage you can do with a shotgun. You think I want my truck window shot out again?"

"You remember that?"

"How could I forget?" He bent down and kissed her lightly on the lips. The fireflies were dancing in the darkness. The stars filled the clear sky and the moon was so close you could almost reach up and touch it. Of course, Willow didn't notice a thing.

Chapter 6

The next morning Willow hummed to herself as she drove to the ice cream shop. In fact, a few times she sang out loud. And she giggled. Like a school girl. She didn't care who killed Clancy. Well, maybe she did. But, it was the last thing on her mind. She burst through the back door singing "I'm Walking on Sunshine" as loud as she possibly could.

Janie peeked through the kitchen door. "What on earth is going on?"

"I'm happy." Willow beamed.

Janie scowled. "Weren't you involved in another murder?" She draped a dishtowel over her shoulder and looked at her with mild curiosity. "And what are you doing up so early?"

"Involved? I would hardly call it involved. Innocent bystander is more like it. And sleep? Who could sleep on such a beautiful morning?" A crash of thunder interrupted their banter.

Janie looked out the kitchen window. Storm clouds. "Who drugged you?"

Willow pressed her hand against her heart. "I'm wounded."

"Ha! Never mind. You were with Steve last night, weren't you?"

"Maybe." Her smile nearly split her face.

The front door jingled and Janie looked behind her. "Speak of the devil."

Willow quickly looked in the mirror and tamed a few stray auburn hairs while Janie went out front to greet Steve. His presence always made her stomach flutter. She wasn't sure if this was normal behavior for a 43 year old, but since when had she ever been normal?

She sucked in her cheeks trying to look stoic. It didn't work. Her eyes were still dancing. She allowed her smile to follow suit. Willow loaded a tray with mugs, a fresh pot of coffee, muffins, and their new menu items of bacon Swiss, and asparagus gruyère quiches to the table. And Janie wanted to know why she was in so early. She should have guessed!

Her smile was still in place when she placed the tray in front of Steve.

"What's this?"

"It's a surprise. We've added quiche to the menu." Willow set the table then placed a bacon quiche in front of Steve and the asparagus gruyère in her spot. "You can have a bite of mine if you'd like to try this one." She poured them coffee then sat down and took a bite.

Steve didn't say a word until he was a few bites in. "This is delicious." He stuck his fork in her quiche. "It's good. I'll stick with the bacon though."

Willow nodded. She'd known what his favorite would be from the get go.

Steve pushed his chair back after finishing his breakfast. "I just realized, you're here." He glanced at his watch. "Willow, it's 10 o'clock. What is wrong with you? You normally don't come in until lunch time."

"If I don't come in during the morning lull, I'll miss out on this. We'll be out by lunch."

"So, food is enough to get you going in the morning?" He looked to Janie. "Why hasn't anyone told me this before now?"

Janie shrugged. "It's not always food. And it won't be quiche for long. Pretty soon she'll realize she's the boss and can have us put one away for her." Janie winked at Willow.

"Why didn't I think of that?" She took the last bite of her breakfast then slowly savored her coffee. Now that her stomach was satisfied, her mind quickly returned to the murder victim. "Steve, how well did you know Clancy?"

Steve started laughing. "Nothing like interrogating the police chief."

"I just thought you might know why five different people broke into his house yesterday. He can't have that many secrets, can he?"

"We all have secrets." He stared intently for just a second before allowing a slight grin.

Willow blushed. On more than one occasion Steve had asked about Embry's dad. She had successfully changed the subject each time with ease. At least she had thought so. She wasn't ready to open that can of worms. Someday, just not yet. She sat silently, waiting for him to answer.

"Clancy bought the cabin across the lake shortly after my grandparents did. Dad always taught us to be respectful of him and our mother, our teachers, our pastors, people in authority—police officers, firemen etc., elders in general, and men who served our country. So when Clancy moved in, we had a real life hero living a stone's throw away from us. We had him over for weekend barbecues and eventually, he became a friend, especially to my dad."

"So, you aren't aware of any dark secrets? Anything at all to tarnish his hero reputation?"

Steve shook his head. "No, nothing serious. I'd caught him changing his story a few times but I chalked it up to getting older and being forgetful. He'd had some problems way back when with a woman, my dad told me the basics. But we never held it against him. War does crazy things to people."

Willow looked around. Business was slow this morning. It wouldn't be long before the lunch crowd would start filtering in. For now, they had the place to themselves. "Had you met Abel before? He appeared out of nowhere. I didn't see him at the range and he wasn't part of our gun club. I'm not sure how he came to be there."

"I had never met him before. Apparently they've been friends for a while. Even served together. What did his granddaughter say? Exactly?"

Willow explained how fraught the girl had been and told him what she said. "I was going to ask her why she thought her grandfather murdered Clancy, but he came back and they left before I had a chance. I would really like to chat with her."

Willow added a dose of steaming coffee to her cup. She inhaled deeply. "I think I need a nap."

Steve, who had just taken a drink from his own cup, snorted coffee up through his nose. "A nap? You just got up."

"What? Clover kept me up all night. I think there's a coyote hanging out at our place and it's driving her mad." She lifted her sandaled foot up. "Besides, every time my toe hit the covers, I would yelp in pain. So maybe I was keeping Clover up."

Steve and Janie leaned over to look at Willow's toe. Both made a face. Her big toe was nearly twice the size it should have been, red, and oozing nasty.

Janie just shook her head. She'd tried to get her to the doctor and it didn't work.

Steve wasn't taking no for an answer. "Janie, what time do you leave? This girl's going to the doctor."

Willow protested. "I have to work."

"I'll call in a part-timer to help this evening. We'll be fine." Janie turned to Steve. "If you can get her to the doc, I'll give you free coffee and muffins for a week."

"Hey. That's my coffee and muffins you're promising."

Janie ignored Willow. "She'll never know. She'll be sleeping."

Steve stood up. "Come on. Let's go."

Willow scowled but stood up. She'd done such a good job hiding how terrible her toe actually was. She mumbled. "How embarrassing. Who gets an ingrown toenail?"

Steve turned. "What did you say?"

"I'm coming." She hobbled after him.

A half hour later she was sitting in urgent care biting the inside of her lip. "This is gonna hurt."

Steve tried to console her. "You've been walking around in pain for the last three months. Don't think I didn't notice. It'll feel better before you know it."

The doctor walked in with a needle kit. A long needle kit. He looked her toe over. "I'm going to make sure this is really good and numb before I start cutting the nail away. You won't like me much tomorrow, but today you won't be feeling any pain, OK?"

She nodded. She knew she needed to deal with this darn toe. She'd been hoping she could do the deed herself. But every time she started to touch the toe, she'd cry out in pain. It just wasn't happening.

The doctor inserted the needle between her toes. "This should take care of it. I'll be back in 15 minutes or so and we'll see if you're numb."

As promised, the doctor returned. "OK, close your eyes." He touched her toe and she jerked it away.

"Ouch."

He pulled out the needle. "I'm gonna have to go straight in under the toe nail. This isn't going to be pleasant."

Willow sat perfectly still.

"Can you feel that?"

She nodded, her face turning a few shades of white.

The doctor raised his eyebrows. "You are tough."

"Doc, this must be your favorite procedure."

"Hmm…well, I like one better– bowel obstructions. Those are my favorite." He grimaced. "In fact, my first day as an intern, the residing took a look at my hands and said, 'you'll do' then told me to find some gloves. Best way to start my career. Let me tell you that was a fun day."

Willow laughed. Maybe toes weren't the worst. A close second, but definitely not the worst.

Five shots later and a toe that had turned white from so much numbing medication, the doctor finally began cutting away the toenail. She didn't watch the procedure. She didn't have to. The faces Steve was making was enough to know it was gruesome.

"I'm going to send you home with a prescription for some pain meds. You should be numb for a while with all the shots I gave you but tomorrow you're going to be hurting."

She nodded and hobbled out on her wrapped foot.

Thirty minutes later they were in the drive up line at the drugstore when her toe started throbbing.

Willow perched in her recliner with her foot up and downed two pain pills. Within minutes, she started getting loopy and her eyelids began to flutter. She smiled at Steve. "I love your dimples."

He grinned but didn't say a word.

Her snoring started out like a small kitten's purr. An hour later when Embry showed up, she had turned into a lion. "Mom's gonna be so embarrassed tomorrow."

Steve headed for the front door. "She won't be if you don't tell her."

Embry grinned. "Yeah. Not going to happen."

Steve chuckled. "You are mean. Janie will be here a little after 2 and I'll be back to relieve her at 6. You work till late, right?"

"I'll be here as soon as I get cut. Might not be until midnight or so."

"That's OK. I'll hang out with gimpy. We can watch a movie."

"If I know mom, she'll be trying to solve a murder."

Steve shook his head. "Try to talk her out of it, will ya?" He waved and headed to his truck.

Dinner was nearly ready when Embry heard moans coming from the recliner. "Mom, you're awake."

Willow barely glanced at her daughter. "This is killing me. I need my pain pills."

Embry glanced at her watch. "You've got another hour before you get more." The look on her mother's face caused her to slowly back up. "OK, OK, I'll get them." She handed her mother one pill.

Willow snatched the bottle out of her daughter's hand and added a second pain pill to her mouth then lowered the footrest on the recliner. "Ow. Ow. Ow." She muttered the entire way to the bathroom.

When she returned, Embry had a streaming bowl of Zuppa Toscana with a large chunk of Italian bread on a television tray next to Willow's recliner. Willow sniffed it appreciatively. Even in pain she was thankful for good food. "How long have I been sleeping? When did you get here?" She looked around the room. "Where did Steve go?"

"Well, he decided it wasn't appropriate for the town's police chief to spend the night with his main squeeze, so he called me."

"Oh, tell me he didn't say that."

Embry's devious smile told Willow absolutely nothing. "You better eat. Those pain pills are going to knock you out again."

Willow scowled. "He did not say that. I know better." She perked up. "Did he say anything about Clancy?" She stared at her wrapped toe. "This could have waited. How can I think clearly with these drugs in me?"

"You can't. Maybe he did this on purpose to keep you from getting into trouble?"

"No, he wouldn't do that, would he?"

Willow woke up in pain. *Darn toe.* She hobbled to the bathroom. Clover was sticking close. She knew something was wrong and she was scared to death that Willow was beyond repair. At least that was Willow's guess by how her dog was behaving. She petted the dog's head. "I'm all right, Girl. Just a little bump in the road. I'll be throwing you sticks before you know it."

Embry was sleeping soundly on the other side of her bed, just in case Willow needed her during the night. She scooped up her pain pills and phone, then quietly closed the bedroom door as she exited.

Willow made a couple pieces of toast and poured herself a glass of milk. The pain pills seemed to settle better with food in her stomach. She carefully propped herself up in the recliner and went through her phone messages while Clover snored softly by her side. Poor dog's schedule was so messed up.

Willow smiled at Janie's text. *I've got quiche for a late lunch tomorrow. Don't eat before I come. I'll be there a little after two. Hope your toe feels better.*

She decided not to text her back. She glanced at the time. After 4. Then again, she did get an early start at the ice cream shop. She punched in a quick reply. *Toe hurts like a bugger. Quiche sounds great. See you tomorrow.*

After reading texts, she listened to her voicemail. *Jordina? How did she get my number?*

Willow listened carefully. "Mrs. Crier." Willow would have to fix that little error when she talked to the girl. There was no Mrs. Crier. "I need to talk to you. It's important. Meet me, please. Tomorrow. 7 p.m. At the library." The phone call ended as abruptly as it began.

Chapter 7

Willow's toe was throbbing. By the time Janie left and Steve showed up, she'd been off her pain medication for nearly 12 hours. Her last dose had been 4 a.m., just before she listened to her voice messages. *Now the hard part—talking Steve into taking me.* She was counting on the lawman in him to be the slightest bit curious as to why one of their suspects wanted to talk to her. She crossed her fingers.

Her stomach grumbled.

"You hungry?"

She pasted her sweetest smile on. "Yeah. I'd kind of like to get out of the house though. Want to grab a burger?"

He studied her as if he knew something was up. "You're supposed to be resting. I'm surprised you're not sleeping."

She glanced at her toe. "It's doing much better. Really. If you aren't hungry for a burger, how about we run over to the library in a little while. I wouldn't mind getting a book to read." She pointed to her chair. "If I'm going to be in that thing for another day or two, I need something to do besides watch TV."

"What's really going on?"

She slunk down in her chair, defeated, and played the voicemail for Steve. After it finished, she looked up at him and frowned. "Just to the library, I promise. Then we'll come straight back here where I'll remain with my foot up. And I'll take my pain pills so I can get some rest. I'll be good."

Steve blew a long breath out. Willow couldn't help but notice as she was waiting for his answer. She remained quiet. She was at his mercy and she knew it. Unfortunately.

"OK. I'll take you. Do you still want a hamburger out? We could run by Molly's café. I'm sure she will spoil you rotten. Being injured and all."

Willow jumped up and instantly regretted it. "Ouch…ow. Oh, my stupid toe." She hopped around on one foot until the pain subsided then threw her arms around Steve's neck. "Thank you! I promise I'll share everything she tells me."

He pushed her back. "You won't have to. I'll be right there with you."

"But…but…" she stammered.

"No buts about it. If we're going to see what a potential murderer has to say I'll be with you." He gave her foot a quick glance. "Besides, what if she decides you know too much. You can't even run."

"She's not the murderer and you know it. If anything, she's trying to protect her grandfather." Her stomach grumbled. "And yes, dinner sounds divine. Molly's is perfect. But, let's eat after."

Willow slipped one foot in her sandal. Her other foot was too swollen and even the thought of trying to put a shoe on sent pain ripping up her leg. She shuddered.

"Perhaps we should reschedule."

"No, I'm fine, really." She hobbled out the front door then turned to Clover. "Hold down the fort, Girl. I'll bring you a treat back."

Steve dropped Willow off in front of the library then found a parking place.

Willow slowly made her way to the front door, wincing in pain with each step. She sure hoped Jordina had something useful to share. A whole day with no pain meds was taking its toll. She was fighting tears the pain was so bad. She couldn't let Steve see just how much it hurt. If she did, he'd make her head back home. She opened the front door and was greeted by the librarian, Mrs. Peterson.

"Willow dear, what happened to you?"

Willow looked down at her foot, which was wrapped in white gauze. "Ingrown toenail. They had to cut away the nail. Hurts like a bugger." Willow tried to walk through the front door but Mrs. Peterson blocked the way. She kept making funny gestures with her eyes.

"What?"

"You're not looking at the sign."

Willow was getting irritated. "What sign?"

"No shirt, no shoes…" she looked down at Willow's shoeless foot, "…no service."

"I can't get a shoe on my foot, Mrs. Peterson."

"I'm sorry. The rules are for everyone."

Steve jogged up to the dueling duo. "What's going on?"

Willow turned to him. "She won't let me in."

Mrs. Peterson tilted her chin up and crossed her arms in front of her. Willow was surprised she didn't dig in her heels while she was at it. "The rules are the rules. You better than anyone should understand that, Steve."

He nodded. "I do understand." He glanced at her feet and shrugged. "I'll be right back." He took off jogging again for his truck. A few minutes later he returned. "Think you can slip this on?"

At first, Willow could only stare. She looked from the rubber pants to Steve and back to the pants. "You have to be kidding me?"

He looked at his watch. "If you want to get in the library, this is probably your best bet."

She held up the oversized pair of fishing waders and gulped. She thought about Jordina waiting inside. She thought about Clancy, a war hero, no longer among the living. She thought about sweating off some of the Jell-O attached to her thighs. "OK. I'll do it."

Willow gingerly inserted her foot into waders. She cried out in pain a few times but doggedly persisted. The other foot was easy going and before she knew it, she was chest high in rubber pants with suspenders. She was so thankful she did not have a mirror handy. She did not want to know how ridiculous she looked. Ignorance was bliss.

Mrs. Peterson held the door open wide. "Now, that wasn't too hard, was it?" She waddled alongside Willow and made small talk, like visiting the library in a pair of waders was an everyday occurrence.

Willow entered the library slowly, the squeak of the rubber with each step gave her pause. The quiet of the library accentuated the rubber meeting rubber sound which was hard to avoid.

Mrs. Peterson turned and put her finger to her lips. "Shhh… This is a library."

Willow stopped. "Really?" She said without lowering her voice.

Mrs. Peterson pursed her lips, then continued walking.

As the small group progressed, Willow felt her face heating up. Each person they passed stopped what they were doing and stared at her. Some giggled. Some pointed. Most had an expression that begged an explanation. Some even asked, "Was the bathroom flooding? Did the sewer back up? Was there some sort of fishing demonstration planned for this evening? If so, which room?"

Steve was doing everything he could to avoid laughing. If the teeth marks left on his index finger were any indication of just how difficult that was, well, his task was nearly impossible. When Willow told one group of ladies she'd already lost an inch off each thigh and perhaps they should give it a go, he busted. He could no longer hold it in.

Willow didn't bother looking at Steve. She kept her head held high, as well as those size 12 boots— those required giant purposeful steps or she would have been tripping over her own bandaged foot which would have in turn assured the library patrons quite the show. One giant rubber duck, at your service.

Chapter 8

Willow wondered if Jordina would show. After all this, she truly hoped so. She made her way to the mysteries and found Agatha Christy—their agreed upon meeting place—and perused the titles. She heard a small voice clear behind her. Steve was standing in the next aisle over. Willow had convinced him Jordina might talk more freely if he wasn't directly part of the conversation.

Willow turned around. "Jordina, you made it."

She nodded. The fact that the girl didn't look twice at Willow's get up proved she was worried beyond reason.

Willow raised her eyebrows. "You asked me to meet you. Was it to explain what you said at the gun range?"

Jordina's eyes filled with tears. "Mrs. Crier, my grandpa killed Clancy. I don't know what to do."

"How do you know he killed him? And why would he want him dead?" She inserted, "And please, call me Willow. Mrs. Crier was my mother."

Tears were staining the beautiful young woman's cheeks. "Clancy didn't earn that Medal of Honor, not really. My grandpa saved those men in Vietnam, not Clancy. By the time Grandpa was able to report what had happened, Clancy had already taken credit. He had been presumed dead and was in a hospital, in a coma, and no one knew who he was. By the time Grandpa woke, Clancy had already been heralded as a hero. When Grandpa confronted him, Clancy asked him who they were going to believe, a white man or black man, then he laughed. My grandpa knew he was right. They weren't going to believe him. He always said in his heart he knew what really happened and that Clancy got his reward here on Earth and he would get his in heaven."

"If that was really his attitude then why do you think, after all this time, he wanted revenge now? And why was he and Clancy even friends? That doesn't make sense."

Jordina wiped her eyes. "I don't know why, but it has to be him." She glanced down the row of books. "They weren't friends. Grandpa always says, 'keep your friends close, and keep your enemies even closer.' That would make him an enemy, right?"

Willow wondered. She'd spent time with Clancy. While he pretended to be modest about his Medal of Honor, he wasn't too modest. If prodded he had no problem sharing his bravery. The vivid description of exactly what happened, and the fact that he told the same story with no deviation, pretty much gave credence to his account. But, if he had witnessed what happened, he would have just as detailed information as if he had been involved. "I don't know. I think we need to speak with your grandfather. He'd be the one to shed some light on the whole situation."

Jordina put her hand on Willow's arm. "Do we have to? He's the only family I have. When my parents died, he took me in and raised me. What's he going to think? That I would turn on him?"

Willow smiled. "No, he wouldn't expect anything less of you. He raised you to be trustworthy and truthful, to have values and morals. He would probably be upset if you hadn't come to us."

Jordina looked around. "Us?"

Steve walked around the corner. "Hi Jordina. We met briefly the other day. I'm Steve."

She nodded then looked at Willow inquisitively.

"He wouldn't bring me if I didn't let him listen in. Besides, it's his job and I have to do the right thing too." She shrugged.

"Jordina, we'll do everything we can for your grandfather. He sounds like a good man. We'll get to the bottom of this."

She pulled a piece of yellowed newspaper from her pocket. "I found this in Grandpa's room. I thought you should see it." She turned to leave.

"Jordina?" Willow called after her.

"Yes?"

"What were you doing at Clancy's cabin?"

Jordina's face paled. "How did you know about that?"

Willow remained quiet.

"I…I…" She stuttered, "I just wanted to see if there was any evidence incriminating my grandfather. That's all." She turned and quickly left.

Willow turned to Steve. "Well, what do you think?"

"I think we have more questions than we do answers. Before we go searching for them, we need to get something to eat. I'm starving."

Willow squeaked her way back through the library and climbed into the passenger seat of Steve's truck. "I'm going to take my pain pills as soon as I get something to drink."

An hour later, after their stomachs were full and Willow's pain pills were giving her cause to smile again, she settled into her recliner.

Within minutes, Embry and Marshall popped in. Embry's smile nearly blinded Willow. She glanced at her watch. "Hi, Marshall, what brings you out tonight?"

Marshall immediately dropped to one knee. "Ms. Crier, do I have your permission to marry your daughter?"

Embry cleared her throat and Marshall turned to look at her. She was indicating he should stand up, with both her eyes and her hands.

"Oh, oh, yes, I'm sorry." He quickly stood up and re-asked the question. "I would like to marry your daughter. Do we have your blessing to get married?"

Willow looked from her daughter to Marshall and back again. She was thankful she'd taken two pain pills. She stood up and hugged her daughter to her and whispered. "Is this what you want?"

Embry pulled back and with tears, nodded.

Willow kissed her cheek. "Then congratulations, my sweet girl. I'm so happy for you!" She turned to Marshall. "Looks like I'll finally have a son. Yes, you have my blessing."

Chapter 9

Steve left after congratulating the engaged couple. Marshall followed shortly thereafter. Embry giggled. "Mom, I'm getting married. Can you believe it?" She held out her hand. "Look. Isn't it beautiful?"

Willow held her daughter's delicate hand in her own and gazed at the beautiful diamond engagement ring. "Oh honey, it's just gorgeous."

Even loopy Willow enjoyed spending the evening listening to Embry share all her ideas about the wedding. They would have so much to do. The young couple wanted to marry in just over a year. It seemed so far off but in reality, they would just have enough time to get everything planned. They wandered from one topic to the next, landing on the reception and the food.

Yawning, Embry asked, "Speaking of food, have you perfected your fried chicken recipe yet for the state fair contest?"

Willow nodded her head. "Almost. I've got a little more prep work to do. I can't believe that we're getting so close. Next weekend already." She picked up her notebook. "I've pretty much got all the ingredients tweaked, just a couple more run-throughs and I'll be good to go." She looked up. "You're coming, right?"

"Wouldn't miss it for the world." She yawned again. "You ready for bed?"

"Yeah, and you don't have to sleep in my bed tonight. You really don't have to stay at all. I can manage now without 'round the clock care."

"I'm staying. One more night, just in case." Embry jumped up. "I almost forgot." She rummaged around in her overnight bag. "I brought you a present. When Steve texted me that picture of you in those waders, I stopped and picked up some open toe sandals."

"He didn't!"

"It was in your best interest, honest. He asked me if I had any sandals you could borrow so you wouldn't have to wear rubber pants out and about." She bent down and kissed Willow. "So, are you next?"

Willow was confused. "Next?"

"You and Steve. Are you next?"

"Goodness no. I'm not sure I'll ever be ready to go down that road."

"Mom…" She smiled. "You'll change your mind. I'm sure of it." She kissed her mother on the cheek. "Sweet dreams. I know I will."

The next morning Willow was up and about before Embry. *Probably too excited to sleep.* Embry had the day off and Willow needed her daughter's help, so she fried up some bacon then added sausage to the pan for gravy. "That'll wake her up." Willow had plans for the day and Embry played a big part in those plans. At least in the transportation department. She couldn't drive on pain pills and no way was she going without. Not after the day before.

The biscuits were nearly done before Embry came stumbling out of the bedroom. "This isn't fair."

"Oh, I'm sorry. Was I being too loud?"

"Yeah, right." She breathed in the luscious southern breakfast food. "I guess there are worse ways to wake up."

Willow slid two scrambled eggs onto her plate.

"Mom?"

"Yeah."

"What do you want?"

"Not much. Just a chauffeur."

"I've been in that position before. I almost got run off the road and shot at, remember?"

"This is different. I promise."

Embry rested her head in her hands then looked up. "Where are we going?"

"Back to the scene of the crime."

Embry leaned back against the chair. "I should have known.

Chapter 10

Willow tried the doors of the building. "Locked." She turned around and gave the "you're in trouble" look to Embry who had refused to get out of the Jeep. "I'm the chauffeur, remember?" She mimicked her daughter's reminder. Outside was all she was going to get. She'd have to be happy with that. *I suppose, it wouldn't be too smart to leave a gun range open willy-nilly.*

She trudged around to the back of the building. The police really had done a good job of collecting the evidence, even the cigarette butts were gone. Willow decided to expand her search. The woods behind the building would be a great hiding place if you were waiting for someone to step out for a smoke. She walked the perimeter.

"Ah ha!" She bent down and picked up several cigarette butts from the ground just inside the trees. She wondered if they would be a match to any found on the scene. She put them in a little baggie— she'd grabbed several before leaving the house. She tried to remember who all went out back to light up. And who would know Clancy was a regular.

Willow climbed in the passenger seat. "OK, onward my good chauffer."

Embry sighed. "I should be home looking at wedding magazines."

"Oh, you will be soon enough. We have a killer to catch." Willow gave directions to Embry and sat back and closed her eyes. She only took one pain pill to avoid being put to sleep.

"Mom, I think we're here."

Willow opened her eyes. "Oh, yeah. Pull up there on the side of the road."

Embry did as she was told. "Now what?"

"Now, we investigate. Birdie parked here and walked through the woods. I thought we'd follow her same steps."

"Why don't we just pull in the driveway? It's not like she was looking for anything out here." She added. "Besides, you're gimpy and you're afraid of snakes. Did you see all the tall grass? You aren't even wearing boots."

"You've got a point. The driveway it is."

Willow jiggled the door handle. She noticed Embry didn't put up a fuss this time about getting out of the Jeep. *Nosy girl.* "It's locked."

"And this surprises you?"

"I guess not." She walked around the perimeter of the house, trying to peek in windows. "Steve would know how to get in." She muttered.

[65]

She was looking in the back window and let out a yell. Standing on the inside waving to her was Embry. She ran around the front.

"How did you get in?"

Embry held up a key. "Steve gave it to me. He said it might keep you out of trouble."

"The nerve of that man. I can't believe…" She paused. "…well, maybe I can. Let's look around."

"Someone was going through his recipes." Embry held the index card holder up.

"That's hardly reason to kill a man. There has to be something else."

Willow hobbled into the office. A scrapbook was on the desk so she leafed through the pages. Several pages had empty spots where something had been on display. She paused on a page with a much younger Clancy posing with a woman who looked like Birdie. *Weird. Birdie is much younger than Clancy.* She turned the page. She knew the local police were questioning each of the four suspects about their visit to Clancy's cottage. She would love to see those reports.

She opened what she thought was another scrapbook and instead she found his checkbook— one of those in a three ring binder. All the checks stubs had payee information and amounts except the last one. The check was missing and the stub was blank. "That's weird. He seems to be meticulous in keeping track of his spending. Why wouldn't he have recorded this check?"

When Embry didn't respond, she walked into the living room to see her hands raised in the air and a uniformed police officer with his gun drawn. Willow immediately stopped moving and put her hands up too. "Um, Sir, we have permission to be here."

The young police officer kept switching who he was pointing the gun at. "Just stay where you are. We'll figure this out when back up arrives."

Willow started to sweat, just a little. Her gun was concealed in her purse. She didn't want to freak the young police officer out any more than he already was but duty to reveal she had a firearm propelled her forward. "Officer, I have a gun in my purse."

"A gun?" He nearly shrieked. "Get down on the floor, both of you. Now."

Both Embry and Willow dropped to the floor. Willow tried to explain. "I have a permit. It's in my wallet. If you'd just let me show you…"

"I hope they lock you two up and throw away the key. To think you'd kill an American hero like that."

Willow glanced at Embry who was glaring at her. She mouthed, "What did I do?"

By the time back up arrived, Willow was lying on the floor facedown, handcuffed and Embry's wrists were constrained with a zip tie.

One of the higher ranking officers asked, "Parker, what have you done?"

"Sir, she has a gun."

"Son, half the state of Oklahoma has a gun. Did she pull it on you?"

"No, Sir. She told me she had a gun." The perspiration beaded up on his forehead revealed just how nervous he was.

"Take the cuffs off them and help them to their feet."

"But Sir…"

"No buts about it, Parker. Do it."

The young officer undid the hand restraints and helped Willow and Embry to their feet. He mumbled under his breath and walked away.

Willow muttered right back at him.

"Sorry about that. He's new to the force. I had him watching the house just in case another suspect showed up." He looked at the rookie who seemed to be apologetic. "He wasn't supposed to engage until back up arrived." He turned back to Willow. "I guess his good intentions got the best of him. I'm guessing you're Willow, Steve's friend.

Thanks for your help the other day. We couldn't have narrowed down the suspects without your help."

Willow fought the urge to give the young cop a dirty look. "You're welcome. I consider it my civic duty to help." She showed him what they found.

"We know who took the missing articles but, we missed the blank check. It could be something, or it might not. But, we'll look into it. Did you find anything else?"

"No, we didn't have time. I'd like to look around a little bit more, if that's OK with you."

"Sure go ahead."

"Did you find a copy of his will?"

"Yes and no. We didn't find it but we do have a copy— got it from his lawyer. Jason, his young employee, was set to inherit everything but Clancy made out a new will with his lawyer right before he was killed. You'll never guess who inherits now."

"Who?"

"Jordina, Abel White's granddaughter. We have no idea why. It doesn't exactly make sense."

"What is his estate worth?"

"With everything, a little over 2 million bucks."

Willow whistled. "I wonder if Jordina knew about it." And to herself she thought, *she just ended up on the top of the suspect list.*

Chapter 11

Willow stood at the kitchen sink and rinsed their breakfast dishes. Embry had been silent the entire drive home. She'd been upset. That was understandable, but the whole fiasco hadn't been her fault. Besides, if the police hadn't of shown up she wouldn't know about the change in the will. Jordina really did have a motive for murder, even if she played innocent, pointing the police toward her grandfather to cover her own guilt. Willow sighed. She would have to ween herself off the pain pills if she was going to do any more snooping. She doubted she'd be able talk Embry into taking her any time soon.

She looked through the freezer. Comfort food. That's what she needed. She pulled out the pint-size ice cream container. She'd stopped bringing the gallon-size home. She'd eat it all. She dipped her spoon in the mocha ice cream. A new flavor for the shop and it was heaven. Tomorrow she'd wear her new sandals and take herself to work. Tonight, she was having dessert first. She turned on Midsomer Murders and settled in for a good whodunit.

About 5 minutes into the show, Clover started barking. Willow peeked out the front door. Steve. She opened the door for him then sat back down with her ice cream. Commiserating with each spoon full she shoved in.

"Are you in here pouting?"

"No. Well, maybe. Just a little though. I was, then I wasn't. I guess I got caught up in thinking over the suspects. Ice cream always makes me feel better."

He smiled. "Can I have a bite?"

She fed him a spoonful.

He closed his eyes and savored the sweet treat. "You're right. I feel better already." He looked around. "Did you eat supper yet? Or is this your supper?"

"I was thinking about heating up some leftover soup. Want some?"

"I've had a chuck roast cooking in my crock pot all day for some French dips. You interested?"

Willow smiled. "I'm pretty sure you already know the answer." She put the lid back on and stuck the remainder of the ice cream in the freezer. "Want some help?"

"Nope. I think you've done enough for today. Sit back down. I've got this." Steve ran to his truck and returned with his crock pot. The aroma nearly bowled her over. Willow got out of her chair, hobbling towards the kitchen.

Steve looked up. "I thought I told you to sit down and rest."

She waved her hand, cutting off any future protests. "I just need to use the ladies' room!" Her voice trailed off as she walked to the bathroom.

Suddenly he heard a piercing scream.

Steve ran towards the bathroom and pushed the door open with a crash. Willow was in the tub, as far away from the toilet as possible. He leaned over and saw a small snake floating in the toilet bowl. A small *plastic* snake. Steve laughed. Uncontrollably. Willow turned to glare at him as he got ahold of himself and reached to help her out of the bathtub.

"What is so funny!?" She exclaimed.

Steve reached for the toilet brush and used it to lift the lifeless snake from the water. "Why don't you asked Embry," he muttered, trying hard not to laugh again. "You might have deserved this one."

Steve went back to the kitchen, leaving Willow to stew, knowing that food would settle her down. Steve pulled the roast out of the hot liquid and sliced the meat, or tried to, as it fell apart. He removed most of the liquid and put it on the stovetop to reduce. While that was working, he buttered the rolls and toasted them on the griddle.

After a lengthy reprimand for Embry, Willow hung up the phone then answered the call of her growling stomach. She could no longer ignore the aroma that filled her house. The smells wafting from her kitchen were giving her belly many reasons to out and out protest.

When the buns were finished Steve placed some chopped roast on the griddle and melted both Mozzarella and Provolone cheese over it before adding it to the buns. She listened to him whistle as he moved from stove top to table and back again, the sizzle of the cheese adding rhythm to his melody.

Finally, after what seemed an eternity, he placed a plate before her. Willow dipped her sandwich in the steaming liquid, then took a bite. She made several noises, none of them intelligible. After swallowing she asked, "How did you learn to cook like this? This is incredible."

He smiled. "I've been single for nearly 45 years. Do you think I always go out to eat or sponge off my sister?"

"You can cook for me anytime. Anytime at all!" She finished her sandwich and wiped her mouth. "And feel free to make these again."

He nodded. "Feeling okay?"

"Yeah. I'm tired. I'm surprised a simple toe procedure took so much out of me."

"Anytime you mess with the body, it's taxing. Even a toe." He tightened his lips. "Can we talk for a few minutes?"

Willow nodded. She knew his serious face by now and he had her concerned.

Steve cleared his throat. "You've never brought up Embry's dad."

She waited for him to go on.

"I imagine he will be coming here for Embry's wedding and I just want to know what I'm going to be up against."

She reached out and took his hand. "You won't be up against anything. Embry's father was never in the picture. I was young and stupid. I loved him. I thought he loved me. Turned out he loved drugs more than me and the baby. I tried to make it work with him, I did. I gave him every chance to step up and be a father. He didn't want the responsibility. To be honest, I've lost track of him. He's never paid a dime in child support. He doesn't have a single picture of his daughter. Not one. He won't show for Embry's wedding. You don't have a thing to worry about. She doesn't have a father."

"Were you two married? Didn't he have a legal responsibility?"

She shook her head. "No. I'm glad too. The whole situation would have only been more complicated." She squeezed his hand. "Everything worked out. He may have had a legal responsibility, but I never pushed the issue. I would never have trusted him with her."

Steve smiled. "Yeah. She's pretty precious. I can understand you doing what you did."

She pulled him close. "And I've never wanted to share her." She kissed him. "Until now."

Chapter 12

Willow felt guilty for being away from the ice cream shop for so long. Three days of playing hooky was enough. She sauntered through the back door. "Hey, Janie, I'm back."

Janie yelled out from the walk in. "I'm taking inventory. Be out in a sec."

Willow helped herself to a muffin. She would have stolen a quiche but she wasn't sure if they were already spoken for. Sometimes customers would order them for pick up. She didn't want to cause her friend any more stress. Having to cover extra hours was enough.

"What are you doing here?"

"I own this place, remember?"

She harrumphed. "Yeah. And I also remember you had a toe procedure and your propensity for doing more than you should sooner than allowed."

Willow gave her a half smile. "I feel useless."

"You're not. You just need to get better."

Two part-timers walked in. Janie addressed them. "Girls, guess I won't be needing you today." They both groaned. Janie smirked.

"Fine. You've got it covered. I get it. I guess I'll run some errands then rest at home. It's getting boring though. A few more days then I'm back, understand?"

Both girls sighed with relief.

Janie walked Willow to the back door. "They both need the money. Stay away for a few days."

Willow sulked back to her Jeep. She turned the air on full blast before closing her door then contemplated her options. Smiling to herself, she pulled out and headed to the city.

Willow rang the doorbell and waited. She rang it again then heard a shout from inside.

"Hold your horses. I'm comin'."

The door swung wide and Birdie's jaw dropped. "Willow? Um, what are you doing here?"

Willow didn't respond. Two things distracted her. First, Birdie was covered in welts. Big ugly swollen welts. Her face. Her arms. Her legs. Pretty much everywhere that wasn't covered by clothing. Second, was Garth, the handy man from the gun range, standing in the living room like he belonged there. Until he saw Willow, that was. Upon seeing who was at the door he went all business like, disappeared into another room altogether then reappeared with what looked like a tool box. He nodded to Willow as he passed her on the front stoop. Without a word to Birdie. That was odd.

Willow found her voice. "What happened to you? And what was Garth doing here?"

Birdie answered Willow's second question first. "Garth was here to fix my stove. I asked him the day of the potluck. Just my luck that it would go out right before the Southern Fried Chicken Cook-Off at the fair. I know my stove so well—I didn't want to have to learn a new one right before the contest—and well, he's so handy, I thought he could fix it for me. Turns out, I thought right. He knew exactly what to do. She stepped aside and invited Willow in.

"As for these red bumps, well, I had a run in with some bees. I'm pretty certain they won."

Oh, that's what happened out at Clancy's. "I'm so sorry. That must be painful."

Birdie paused, as if in thought. "Yes, well, it isn't a picnic, that's for sure. I'm itching all over and it's driving me to drinkin'." She walked away and naturally expected Willow to just follow. Typical Birdie.

Willow thought about beating around the bush then thought better. *Best to just come out with it.* "So, what were you doing at Clancy's the other day?"

Birdie's head jerked up. "What do you mean?"

"The day he was murdered. You were out to his house. Why?"

"Oh, that." Like she had actually forgotten. "I had borrowed his mama's old recipe for biscuits. Best biscuits I ever had. Just wanted to return the recipe before his heirs came a lookin' for it. It's a family secret, or so he said. Wouldn't want to put anyone out."

"Oh. And is that where you…" Willow motioned to the red bumps on her body.

"Yes. I parked a ways away—always thinking about exercise you know—then walked through the woods. It was such a lovely day and I'd just eaten all that fattening food. I thought the walk would do me good. Boy was I wrong about that."

Willow nodded in agreement.

"I already told the police all this. Why are you around asking?"

"Oh, so the police have already questioned you?"

"Sure have. I wouldn't have any reason to hurt old Clancy. I barely knew him."

Willow agreed with her. It wasn't like biscuits was a reason to do anyone in. She changed the subject. "Well, what I really want to know is if you have any pointers for me for the Southern Fried Chicken Cook-Off. I need all the help I can get."

Birdie glanced at her, her eyes narrowing just a little. "You're entering?"

"Yep. Sure am. The only problem is, I wasn't raised on fried chicken."

"So, you've never made fried chicken before?"

"Nope. I mean, I've been practicing at home but I'm doing something wrong. It's just not quite…there."

Birdie slowly nodded. "What method of frying are you using?"

"I bought a deep fryer."

"Huh. Well, that should do the trick. I'm not one to share secrets, especially seeing I'm entering the cook-off myself. I will tell you this much, the judges like simple tried and true fried chicken."

"Is that what you do?"

Birdie's eyes quickly shifted to the kitchen counter then back again. Willow followed suit to see what she had been looking at and Birdie closed the gap and scooped up whatever it was. "Yes, that is exactly what I do. Keep it simple." She walked to the front door and opened it.

Willow took a slight detour when she saw the trophies lined up on the fireplace mantle. "You won all these?" She picked one up and read the inscription. "First Place Cake Bake Off. Wow. I've only won one First Place trophy. Nice." She picked up a second and read it to herself. "You must be a fantastic cook. I didn't think you cooked much since you didn't bring anything to the potluck."

"If you must know I simply ran out of time. Preparing my entries is more important to me than cooking for a potluck."

"Then why'd you go to the potluck? If you were short on time that is."

Birdie stammered then said, "Are you finished? I have things to do and I don't have time for chatting it up with you."

Willow could take a hint. She thanked Birdie for her time and walked to her Jeep. She turned to see Birdie staring at her and waved. Not bothering to wave goodbye, Birdie stepped back in the coolness of her living room and closed the door. "I guess our visit was finished. Simple? Maybe so, but a little help wouldn't have killed her." Thank goodness for friends like Molly. She had several suggestions and Willow was determined to make the best fried chicken she could possibly make.

She stopped at the grocery store, then the butcher's and bought two whole chickens. She had already seasoned her new cast iron skillet. It was true, she had tried the deep fryer but it just didn't produce the results she was looking for. She called Steve, Embry, Janie, and Molly and invited them all for dinner the next evening, a sort of early engagement dinner for her and Marshall. And some much needed practice making her fried chicken. *Chicken is such a fickle thing.* She wished she had spent more time with her grandmother at the kitchen stove. Her fried chicken had been something to swoon over. She sighed.

Upon arriving home, she cut her chicken up then added it to gallon-size freezer bags with her secret marinade. This time she knew she had it right. She could feel it. Once the chicken was in the fridge, she peeled potatoes and put them in cold water and stuck them in the fridge as well. *Might as well get as much done tonight as I can.* After making a hot fudge pudding cake for dessert, she propped her foot up and took a pain pill. She might have overdone it. Well, she did, but then where is the fun in taking it easy all the time?

Willow gave up for the night on trying to figure out why Garth was at Birdie's. Her explanation made some sense, she guessed. The recipe on the kitchen counter which Birdie had tried to hide made her curious. She was running out of partners in crime to go on her breaking and entering road trips. She'd have to figure something out herself.

She made a tuna fish sandwich and settled in her recliner to watch Midsomer Murder when the doorbell rang. Clover was barking up a storm which made Willow wonder who was on the other side. She opened it then nearly choked on her sandwich. Jordina was at her doorstep.

Chapter 13

"Jordina, what are you doing here?"

"I had to talk to you. I just had to."

Willow stepped to the side and invited her in. "Have a seat. Can I get you something to drink?"

The young woman held up her water bottle. "I'm good, thanks." She sat down and crossed her legs at the ankle. She'd certainly been taught manners by someone. Perhaps her grandmother before she had passed on. She quickly pulled a letter out of her pocket and shoved it to Willow, as if the piece of paper was poison. "I found this and knew I had to show it to you. You'll know what to do with it. My heart is just breaking. I love him so much."

Jordina began to cry as Willow opened the letter. Big fat tear drops that certainly conveyed her compassion and hurt over the whole situation. Willow liked the girl more and more. She hoped she wasn't involved in any way. The letter was addressed to Clancy and it was written by Abel.

The letter went on and on about Clancy doing what was right, about him coming forward and telling the truth. Abel also made some pretty heavy handed threats if Clancy didn't do what was expected of him. "Where did you get this?"

"Right after we left the potluck, Grandpa left me at home then took off. He was sweating when he left, like he was worried about something, but when he came home he looked relieved, like he'd worked whatever was wrong out. We got to talking and he was laughing and sharing stories with me. Well, he must have forgotten about the letter in his pocket. When I was doing laundry I came across this letter. When I read it, I knew for certain that my grandfather was at fault. He did this horrible thing. I just know he did."

Willow tried to comfort her. Jordina had lost her parents when she was young, her grandmother as a young teenager, and now it looked as if her grandfather would be going to prison. The poor girl. Willow didn't know what to say. How do you console someone who has been hit so hard by life?

"Will you make sure the police get the letter? It breaks my heart but I had to do the right thing."

"Yes, of course. Are you going to be okay? Is there anything I can do?"

Jordina nodded and started for the door. "There isn't much anyone can do but I'll be all right."

Right before Jordina opened the door Willow said, "One good thing is you won't have to worry about money. Not with you being the primary beneficiary in Clancy's will."

Jordina stopped walking and hastily turned back toward Willow. "Who told you that?"

"The police. You didn't know?"

Jordina studied Willow for a moment before replying. "No, I had no idea. I was asked to come to the reading of the will which is tomorrow after the funeral, but I had no idea why. I guess I found out a little early." The waterworks started back up. "I guess he felt guilty about what he did to my grandpa." She stifled a sob and ran for her car.

Willow watched her leave then called Steve. "I've got something you should probably see." She recounted her visit with Jordina then waited for him to arrive.

After Steve read the letter he shook his head. "I really didn't want this to be true. I like Abel. He's such a good guy. Or at least I thought he was." He shrugged and tucked the letter in his jacket pocket.

Willow was thinking about the whole situation. "I wonder why he waited so long to go after Clancy. Something isn't right."

"Unless something else comes up to say otherwise, I'm guessing there is going to be an arrest tomorrow."

Willow shook her head. "He just doesn't seem the type. I mean, what changes a person? For the first 70 years of his life, he sits back and lets someone else take the credit for a heroic act he performed then all of a sudden, he murders someone. It doesn't make sense."

"I agree with you. But all the evidence is pointing right at him. Who else is there?"

"We haven't spoken with Jason yet."

"No, that's true. But the police have and they haven't found anything to tie him to the murder."

"Well, what about Birdie and Garth? What are they hiding?"

"I haven't a clue. Although I'm sure they're up to something." He considered what he was going to say. "Want to go to the funeral with me tomorrow? Maybe we'll come up with something we haven't thought of before."

"No. I think I've done enough. Embry is just getting over that nonsense at the cabin. If I cancel her dinner she's never going to forgive me.

Besides, the fair is this weekend and I need the practice. If you want to come over after the funeral and fill me in, I'll gladly save you some chicken. Who knows, you might even make it back in time to have dinner with us. We're not eating until 6."

He kissed her nose. "I'm proud of you. I never thought I'd see the day you would turn down attending the funeral of a murder victim."

"Let's just say I'm getting my priorities in order. It's not every day your daughter gets engaged."

"True. Especially if you don't count…"

Willow interrupted. "No, that doesn't count. That was my doing, not hers." She was referring to Embry losing her engagement ring a few months back to distract the murder suspects who had gathered at Willow's house to re-do the chili cook-off. "She wasn't even engaged and there was no ring."

Steve laughed. "I suppose. But you did have a few of our locals going. They were all set for a wedding. I wonder if they'll believe you this time."

She guffawed. "If they look at the rock on her finger they'll know it's for real."

"True." He cozied up to her. "Let's not talk about the case."

"What do you want to talk about?"

[89]

He drew close. Just as he was going in for a real kiss, Clover hopped up between them and starting giving kisses of her own. "Ah, come on, Girl. Can't you share?"

Willow laughed. "She's jealous."

Steve stood and stretched. "I really should be going. I've got to get up early tomorrow. My sister needs help out at the ranch, then I'll head to the funeral then back here."

Willow walked him to the door and smiled when he wrapped his arms around her. Clover jumped up trying to get between them. Steve pushed her away and snuck a quick kiss. "All right, Girl. I'm leaving. You can have her all to yourself." He stepped out on the porch. "I'll see you tomorrow."

Chapter 14

Everyone loved Willow's chicken. The praise was continual all through dinner. Embry seemed to have forgiven her and was all smiles. Willow was thankful. The next morning she was headed to the fair grounds for the Southern Fried Chicken Cook-Off. She had a winner. She was sure of it.

Molly and Janie helped clean up the dishes while Embry was given a pass. The dinner was in her honor. Willow did all the cooking so she was shooed into the living room area with Steve. Finally, they had a moment to discuss the funeral.

"Who all was there? What did I miss?" Willow looked at Steve expectantly.

"It was a full military funeral. He was a hero. The place was packed. All the suspects were there. And you were right about Birdie and Garth. Something is definitely going on there. He came in late and when he finally did arrive he made eye contact with her and nodded. I'm not sure what that was all about. Later I heard someone had broken into the cabin. Your young officer chased them on foot but didn't catch whoever it was. I have my guesses."

"What do you think they were after?" Willow paused. "Garth knows about electrical work. He fixed Birdie's stove."

"It doesn't seem likely it's these two. What could be their motive? Besides, Abel confessed."

She grasped his arm. "What? When?" She stood up. "Why didn't you tell me right away?"

"I thought we'd already come to that conclusion last night."

"That he would be arrested, yes, but not his confession." She paced. "He's covering for Jordina. He has to be. He thinks she did it."

Steve shook his head. "He knew exactly how the killer pulled it off."

"No, he didn't. He doesn't smoke, Steve. I found those cigarette butts just inside the woods, in perfect view of the range. Whoever booby trapped the electrical smoked."

"So we're looking for a guy who both knows about electrical and smokes. But, Jordina doesn't know, she couldn't have done it."

"What about Jason. We still haven't talked to him. We could go tomorrow after the fair. You're still coming with me, right?"

"Of course. I wouldn't miss it for the world." He stroked his chin. "I might have to leave for a little while though." He watched her face fall then added, "I'll be there to help you set up. After that, I've got to run an errand for my sister. But, I'll be back before the judging starts. I promise."

Willow nodded, obviously relieved. This was a one man job so she would be fine doing her thing. She just wanted support. Embry was busy with Marshall's family. Janie would be running the ice cream shop and Molly had her restaurant to take care of. Her chicken was already in its brine and Steve was going to help her load her Jeep before he left. She was in good shape. "OK. You'll be there most of the time. That works. Thank you."

The next morning Steve and Willow drove through the still unpopulated fair grounds. The building being used for the cook-off was just past the animal barns and also used for the 4-H competitions. The Southern Fried Chicken Cook-Off was a special show event put on by some local restaurants. They were providing all the sides and anyone wanting to attend and eat dinner could buy a ticket and have fried chicken and all the fixings— once the restaurant owner judges had their fill that is. All the proceeds were going to fund a local food bank.

She had her portable stove top and her cast iron frying pans. Her chicken had been brined the night before, which was allowed for this competition. Nor did recipes have to be turned in ahead of time. This was a completely "dark" competition. No one had any idea what was coming.

She saw Birdie a couple of stations over and in front of her. She noticed she had one of the turkey deep fryers. In fact, quite a few people did. She patted her trusty cast iron skillet. "You and me. We've got this."

It was noon by the time she and Steve had everything set up. He kissed her cheek. "I'll be back by supper time. Promise." He had parked her Jeep in the side lot and jogged off to go do his errand.

Set up was between 7 a.m. and 2 p.m. The cooking didn't begin until 4 p.m. She had 4 hours to kill. Her stomach rumbled. Of course. Fair food. She smiled and set off to find something good.

She had just polished off an order of chicken and waffles and a bacon cinnamon roll when she spotted them. Jordina and Jason, together, in line at the carousel. They were holding hands and then he kissed her. She tried to remember if she had seen them acknowledge one another at the gun range and the answer she came up with was a big fat no. If they were an item, why would they hide the fact?

She decided to find out. She hurried before their turn came. "Jordina, Jason, I didn't know you two were seeing each other."

Jordina's face turned red and she stammered. Jason tried to ease her discomfort. "With everything going on, we really just started seeing each other. I mean, with Clancy being like a dad to me and her grandfather, and well, what he did, it just seemed natural that we'd turn to one another for comfort. You can't blame us. We've been through the wringer."

Willow nodded. "I guess I'm surprised to see you both here. Clancy's funeral was yesterday…" she turned her gaze upon Jordina, "…and your grandfather has been arrested for murder. Yet here you both are eating cotton candy and in line to ride the Ferris wheel. One would think your world is perfectly right side up."

Jordina was still having trouble speaking, or so it appeared. Jason piped up. "We have both been so stressed out we just needed to step away from it all. We needed a break. The fair seemed the perfect place for that."

Willow nodded. "Well, you both have fun. Jordina, if you find time to see your grandfather tell him I'll be in to see him soon." She turned and walked away before she said something she'd really regret.

Willow re-entered the building where the cook-off was being held just before 3:30. At 4 o'clock she removed her chicken from her cooler and started cutting it apart. For the next hour she battered and fried each piece, letting them cook slowly in the hot oil. Her pieces of chicken had to be on the platter by 6 p.m. She pushed everything else from her mind and worked as quickly as she could. Just before 6 she turned her burners off and removed the hot skillets from the coiled heaters. She would rather have used gas but, electric was as good as it got when the cooking station was mobile.

Steve joined her a few minutes later. "I'm so hungry. When do we eat?"

She smiled at him. "After the judges take their fill. Soon."

It wasn't long before the announcement was made that all participating cooks would start the buffet line. Afterward, everyone with a ticket would be next, and if there was anything left, they would accept walk-ins. Willow put Steve's lanyard around his neck. "You're team Willow."

"Isn't that cheating?"

"Do you want to take the chance they'll have enough for walk-ins?"

"OK boss, whatever you say." He followed her to the buffet line. All the chicken had been placed in large chaffing dishes along with all the sides. All the chicken had been mixed together so no one knew whose chicken they were getting. It was the luck of the draw. And they would be happy with what they got. All proceeds went to charity so those who set up the event figured it wouldn't matter, as long as the food bank had food to carry them through.

Willow loved the fair. She only allowed herself one day to wander the grounds. She wished her metabolism could handle more but her hips didn't lie... and they could not handle more fair food. She glanced at Steve. Perhaps she could talk him into taking a moonlit Ferris wheel ride. She lifted her eyebrows. She'd almost forgot to tell him about Jason and Jordina. "Oklahoma City sure does have some good restaurants." She said as she added loaded mashed potatoes to her plate.

They found a seat at one of the long tables and began to eat. Willow sampled her salads and potatoes before taking a bite of her chicken breast. She closed her eyes and savored the flavor. She'd tasted this recipe before. It was delicious. All of a sudden it dawned on her: this was Clancy's chicken. She looked up from her plate and met Birdie eye to eye. Willow's mouth dropped a little. Birdie looked at the chicken in Willow's hands and flew from the table. Willow was hot on her heels.

Birdie ran out the door. Willow was thankful the woman wore the brightest clothes known to man. Her bright pink T-shirt and capris could be seen zigging through the crowd. Willow's chest felt like it was going to explode but she pressed on. She just kept her eyes on the pink T-shirt. It disappeared in one of the animal barns.

Willow carefully entered the barn. She could hear the squeal of pigs. Steve was right behind her. He pointed to the other end of the barn then disappeared back out the door to cover the other exit. The crowd of people gave her good cover in which to slowly proceed forward without being identified. She glimpsed the pink shirt and started moving a little quicker, hiding behind people when Birdie started to turn her head. That worked great until Birdie neared the other end of the barn and saw Steve. She started to back up then turned and saw Willow. She knew she was caught but she gave it one last ditch effort to escape their clutches and she bounded over one of the fences and into the pig pen. Willow anticipated her move and followed her over, grabbing her by the shoulders and dragging her down in the mud.

A crowd gathered around the two women within seconds, cat calls and whistles could be heard and even teams had formed for the all new "female mud wrestling" championship going on in the pig barn. By the time Willow had Birdie pinned—she did have at least 30 pounds on the woman—the whole barn wanted to know who won. Pigs were running in every direction and both women were completely covered in mud— at least she hoped it was mud.

"You killed Clancy for a recipe?"

"I didn't kill Clancy. I just stole the chicken recipe."

"I don't believe you. And Garth helped you, didn't he?"

Birdie managed to get her legs wrapped around Willow then rolled her. The crowd roared. "I did not kill Clancy!"

Willow was trying to spit mud and…whatever else mixed in…out of her mouth. "I saw those trophies on your mantle. You're obsessed. You killed him for another trophy for your mantle. You knew his chicken was the best you'd ever had and you knew it would take first." She brought her knees up and flipped her long ways over her head. Again, the crowd went crazy.

She quickly sat on her midriff and grabbed her arms. "Admit it. You killed him."

Birdie was twisting and turning, trying to get away. Willow's muddy hands were not effective in keeping her hands pinned so Birdie started flinging mud, anything to distract the woman sitting on her. When she realized it wasn't working, she finally went still. "I didn't kill him, I swear."

Willow stood up and pulled Birdie with her. The crowd cheered and one of her "fans" grabbed Willow's arm and lifted it. "And the winner is... Porkie!" He leaned in and whispered. "Next time you might want to wrestle someone closer to your own weight. I know about these things, I watch plenty of women's wrestling."

Willow grabbed her arm from him and scowled. Willow watched as two police officers led Birdie out of the pig barn. Steve was standing nearly 5 feet away. Each time she moved in closer, he would take a step back. "What is wrong with you?"

He held his handkerchief to his nose. "Nothing," He said sounding like Fran Drescher on steroids.

"Nothing?"

"Well, you do kind of smell. No kind of about it. You need a shower."

She inched closer. "And here I thought we could take a romantic, moonlit Ferris wheel ride."

"Um, maybe later? After you've showered?"

She stood on her tippy toes and kissed him. "I really wanted tonight to be romantic. You could win me a teddy bear, we'd take a ride on the Ferris wheel… maybe share a funnel cake."

I think we need to get you showered up and down to the station. Birdie is threatening to sue and you've got to give your statement.

"Sue? For what?"

Steve raised his eyebrows and gave her the *'are you serious'* look. "You chased her down and tackled her in a pig pen. She's stating you embarrassed her and the damages alone to her psyche are worth thousands."

She shook her head. "That woman is crazy. She murdered Clancy. I'd bet my last dime on it."

"Abel murdered Clancy. He's confessed, Willow. You can't get much surer than that."

Willow stomped off with the smiling couple who volunteered their shower, thankful she'd brought some extra clothes in case she made a mess of herself at the Cook-off. She knew Abel didn't murder Clancy.. She wasn't wrong about this and she'd prove it.

Willow towel-dried her hair then thanked the owners of the RV before stepping out into the early evening heat.

Steve was waiting for her. She smiled and waved goodbye to the older couple then walked back toward the park before asking, "Do you know those people?"

"No. But they sure do know you." He laughed. "They want to know if they can head up your fan club."

Willow sat across from the police officer and tapped her foot. She didn't have time for this nonsense. Finally, after agreeing to stay away from Birdie, as in 100 feet at all times due to a restraining order, she was allowed to go. And, she had to come back and answer for her actions in a court of law.

"You know what I don't get? If she wasn't guilty, why'd she run? Can anyone answer that? She took off. She dropped her plate and bolted. What was I supposed to do? Let her go?"

Steve grinned. "Well, most people would have thought... 'what's wrong with that woman' then went on eating their chicken."

"Obviously I'm not most people."

"Nope, you sure aren't." He added, "Do you want to go back to the fair?"

"No, I think I'll just head home. Another night, maybe."

Chapter 15

Willow decided to go by the gun range. She'd heard a rumor that Clancy had actually left the business to Jason. The rest of his estate went to Jordina. Apparently he'd felt some guilt over what he'd done to her grandfather and tried to make it up by giving Jordina his earthly possessions. And true, some of what he had was because of the benefits he had received being a hero. Many people do kind things for war heroes. She glanced at her clock. *Noon. Steve should be out of church anytime now.*

She heard his truck pull in the driveway and ran out to meet him. "Hey. Ready?"

"Can we get something to eat first?"

She pulled a peanut butter and jelly sandwich out of her purse. "Here, snack on this. We can stop after. Besides, the restaurants are going to be crazy packed. It's Sunday."

He shrugged and devoured the sandwich.

The first thing Willow and Steve noticed was the gun range was open for business and actually busy. Clancy had a pretty faithful following but it was never like this. They had to

park in the field next door. Crazy. Steve opened the door for her and the lobby was packed with enlisted men. Jason must have already let his buddies know about the change in ownership.

They looked around to no avail. Jason wasn't anywhere to be seen. Steve motioned Willow and she followed him down the hallway toward the office she was questioned in. That is where they found him, lip locked with Jordina. At least they assumed he had been since his lips were the same shade as her lipstick.

"Oh, Willow. I'm sorry about yesterday. Really. I thought I was catching something. Turns out I was fine. Must have been my allergies."

Likely story Willow thought before she said, "Well, I'm glad you're feeling better. Maybe now you two can answer some questions for us."

Jason shook Steve's hand. "Good to see you again, Sir." Then nodded to Willow. "Ma'am."

Steve asked, "I couldn't help but notice the place is hoppin'. What's up?"

"We're having a grand re-opening. I've got some local bands set up outside, the range fees are half price, we've got ribs and chicken on the smoker, and we're having a grand prize package drawing of 500 bucks worth of supplies. This is just the beginning. I've got some ideas on bringing new blood to the place. I know Clancy kept it on the down low, but, he could afford to. I'd like to bring some updates, new equipment that sort of thing. Maybe some fresh décor." He pulled Jordina down to him. "Jordina's offered to help me on that end."

Steve was perplexed. "Did you send out a notice to the normal club members? I didn't get one. And I even have email."

Jason looked to Jordina. "That was on your list. Hopefully you didn't forget."

She looked sheepish. "I think I might have."

Jason's face fell. "I'm really sorry about that." He turned to Jordina. "Why don't you send out a quick email? It's still early in the day and we'll be going 'til evening."

She signed in on his desktop and apparently sent the invite.

Willow smiled. He really was a nice guy. Hopefully these two were as upright at they seemed. Willow wasn't so sure. Especially about Jordina. Something wasn't right with that girl. One minute she was upset and claiming her grandfather killed Clancy. The next she was out eating cotton candy and riding carnival rides with her secret boyfriend.

She asked, "So, why did you hide the fact you're in a relationship?"

Jason looked to Jordina who was still messing around on the computer. "I didn't want to hide it, but Jordina thought with everything else going on it might be wise." He continued. "After thinking about it, I decided she was right. We didn't want anyone thinking poorly of us. Nor did we want anyone thinking we had anything to do with Clancy's murder."

Willow asked Jason directly, "Why did you go to Clancy's cabin after he was murdered?"

"I feel really bad about that. He owed me some money and told me he had a check made out to me but forgot it at home. He was getting older and he often would forget things. Anyway, I really needed the money. I already explained that to the detective."

Willow raised her eyebrows toward Jordina. "Does your grandfather smoke?"

Jordina shook her head. "Nope, he used to during the war but he stopped before I was born."

"What about you?"

"Um, yeah, why do you ask?"

She made eye contact with Steve then looked back to Jason. "No reason. Just wondering."

Steve pulled her to the corner of the room and whispered, "I thought you were certain Birdie murdered Clancy."

She whispered back, "I am."

"Then why are we questioning these two?"

"Just to be sure." She shook her head then went back to Jordina. "Are you in possession of Clancy's cabin? And his belongings?"

Jordina nodded.

"If you don't mind, I'd like to get in there. There's something I need to check."

"Well, I don't know about that…"

"Why, do you have something to hide?"

"No, fine, go ahead. I haven't had a chance to go through anything yet so everything he owned should still be there."

"Have you had the locks changed?"

"No," she addressed Steve. "Your key should still work."

Willow climbed in Steve's truck. "I'd like to see Abel. Can you arrange it?"

Steve nodded. "Already done. He can have visitors."

She waited, expectantly.

"Oh, you want to go now? Or after we go to the cabin?"

"I think now. I want him to recant his confession."

"The OKC police are just going to love you."

Willow sat down across from the prisoner. "Abel, I know you didn't kill Clancy."

"Yes, yes, I did. I electrocuted him. I set up those wires to run hot and I pushed him back so he'd step on them. I murdered him, all right. And he deserved it too."

"What if I told you your granddaughter didn't kill him either?"

Abel sat a bit straighter. "Well, of course she didn't. Because I did."

Even though Abel was wasn't backtracking, yet, Willow could see him implore her with his gaze to explain. "I know who killed Clancy. And it wasn't your granddaughter." She looked to Steve who was warning her with a shake of his head. She turned back to Abel. "I need to know, did you really kill him?"

Abel just stared, he didn't say a word.

"Tell me. The police are going to lock you up. You'll never see Jordina fall in love, get married, have your great-grandchildren. You'll never get the attention due you for your service in Vietnam. Your service, the heroic acts you performed and had stolen from you. Why wait all these years to get your revenge? Why now?" She didn't wait for him to answer. "I'll tell you why, because you didn't do it. You didn't kill him and you know it and I know it. The only reason you're here is because you love Jordina more than you love your own life. You know she has a selfish streak and you have no idea how she got it. She may be selfish, she may twist things to get her own way, but she's not a murderer."

He finally spoke. "Can you prove it?"

She nodded. "I believe I can. You need to recant your confession so the police will look further. They won't listen to me with you in here saying you did it."

"I have your word you'll find the real killer and you'll clear Jordina?"

"You have my word."

"Then I'll do it."

Chapter 16

"You have a lot of nerve coming in here and messing with our perp. He's confessed. We have it on tape. You think we're just gonna let him go because he changed his mind?" The detective was not happy with Abel's about-face.

"Even if he didn't do it?"

The officer threw up his hands in exasperation. "And how, pray tell, do you know this? How do you know he didn't do it?"

"Because I know who really did it, that's why."

He crossed his arms. "Does this have anything to do with the woman you chased into a pig pen at the state fair?"

"OK, technically, I did chase her. But she's the one who decided to jump into the pig pen. I just went in after her. And yes, it's her."

"The woman admitted to stealing a recipe. That was her crime. We've already talked to Clancy's heir and she isn't pressing charges. And you'll do well to steer clear of her or you're the one who'll be serving some time in county lock up."

It was Willow's turn to be short on patience. The man wasn't listening. "Fine. If I come in here with evidence, will you at least look into what I find?"

She slammed the door to Steve's truck. "Now we go to the cabin. I need to check something." Just as she suspected, the picture she'd seen in Clancy's scrapbook was missing. The picture with the woman who looked a lot like Birdie with Clancy's arm wrapped around her shoulders. When she saw it the first time she'd paused on it because the woman looked so much like Birdie. Shorter blond hair, obviously a style from the 70's, but if you put a picture of Birdie next to the picture in the scrapbook, the two women could have been twins. Willow suspected that it was actually Birdie's mother.

She and Steve started digging through boxes, searching for a duplicate or another picture of Birdie's mom. Willow needed something to prove Birdie stole more than a recipe.

She called Embry. "Hey, I need you to do an internet search for me. Look up a Garth Weber. I think Garth is his middle name. His first name could be Richard or Dick, I'm not sure. See if there is any connection between him and Birdie Townsend." She paused. "You know what, do a search on both of them and see if you come up with anything. Let me know as soon as you can."

Willow was digging in the office closet while Steve was searching the bedroom.

Steve called out, "Found something."

Willow dropped what she had in her hands and found him kneeling on the bedroom floor.

"Here, take these." He handed her several paper picture envelopes to sort through. He had a few as well.

She quickly scanned the pictures in her piles. "Nothing here. How about yours?"

He shook his head. "There's more boxes up there. Looks like this is where he stored his memories. He's got to have more than that one picture." Steve brought several more boxes from the top shelf.

Willow found a whole box full of old pictures. Most of them were in great condition since they had been protected from the elements for so long. "Bingo." She found an exact duplicate of the picture in the scrapbook as well as a few others, including one of Birdie's mother holding a trophy and a piece of fried chicken. "No!" She held up the picture for Steve to view. "Steve, look at his…" She handed him a picture of Birdie's mom holding a baby. "You don't think…?"

"The only thing I know for sure is I want some answers." He gathered up the pictures, put the boxes back where they found them, and then left. "We'll start with Garth. He's the only one we haven't met with. I want to know what his relationship is with Birdie. Did Embry call you back yet?"

Willow glanced at her phone. "Not yet. But, let's present him with the evidence. He's gonna sing."

"Sing? What crime shows have you been watching lately?" He gave her a sideways glance. "You ever think about becoming a pro? Maybe get your private investigator license?"

"Nah, I'll leave that to you professionals."

He laughed out loud then murmured. "Yeah, that'll be the day."

Just before they arrived at Garth's house, Embry called. "Mom, Garth is Birdie's uncle. As in, her mother's brother."

That little bit of information caused Willow to catch her breath.

"Oh, and something else I found out. Her mother won the Southern Fried Chicken Cook-Off back in the early 70's. Apparently the recipe was handed down and she was going to start up a fried chicken franchise. Something happened and she never got around to it. That was the last time she competed in the cook-off and she won first place. She died shortly after having a baby out of wedlock and the baby was adopted. Birdie's mom's death was mysterious, and foul play was suspected but nothing was ever proven. The father never did step up and claim the baby. Birdie must have found out who her birth mother was and went from there. That would explain why she waited so long to get revenge." Embry paused. "Oh, and Birdie won first place for her southern fried chicken the other day. You don't think…"

Willow didn't know what to think. "It can't be the same recipe, can it?" They finished their conversation and Willow ended the call.

Willow repeated the conversation for Steve. "Do you believe me now?"

They both approached the nondescript grey house with the intention of questioning Garth. As they neared the front door, Garth, whom they both could see clear as day through the front picture window, ran out the back door in a feeble attempt to escape.

Steve said, "Why do they always do that? He's at least 65 years old and out of shape. How far does he think he's going to get?"

Willow simply replied, "Your turn." Then she watched Steve run around the house into the back yard where the man was still trying to climb the chain link fence.

Steve just stood there then cleared his throat.

The big guy stepped away from the fence. "It always looks easier on television."

Steve just nodded his head in disbelief. "Let's go in and talk, shall we?"

They opened the front door for Willow who asked Steve, "Why do you always get the easy ones? Seriously!"

Garth sat down, panting, and out of breath with sweat dripping down his already glistening forehead. "What do you guys want?"

Willow answered. "We wanted to talk to you. Now we want to know why you were running." She rolled her eyes. "What is wrong with people?" She muttered as she waited for Garth to respond. "

"I wasn't running. I was going for a walk, getting some exercise."

"Over a chain link fence?"

"I thought I'd take a shortcut."

Steve waved him off. "Forget it. Let's get down to what is going on with you and Birdie."

"Me… and Birdie?" He stammered. "I don't know what you mean."

"You were at her house the other day, the day I stopped by for a visit. What were you doing there? You left awfully fast when you saw me at the door." Willow tapped her foot.

"I was fixing her television. It went out on her."

"You were fixing her television? The one hanging on the wall above the fireplace?"

He stuttered. "Uh… yeah, I'd just hung it back up when you rang the bell."

She nodded her head. "That's weird because Birdie told me you were there to fix her oven."

Garth's face deepened and his breathing came in short pants.

"Look why don't we help you out? We know you're Birdie's uncle. We've got that much. We know you broke into Clancy's house and stole the picture from the scrapbook." Willow picked up an ashtray. "And I bet if we compared these cigarette butts to the ones we found just inside the woods, I'm betting we'll have a match."

Steve took over. "The job you did for Birdie wasn't on a television or a stove, it was on the wiring at the gun range." He glanced at Willow. "This guy's guilty. He murdered Clancy."

Garth started gasping for breath. "No, I didn't kill him. Birdie did it. I was the look out. I just let her know when he was out there for his smoke break."

Steve corrected him. "You also took care of tampering with the electrical. You willingly and knowingly provided the murder weapon."

"That's all I did, I swear. Birdie's the one who pushed him backward into the live wires."

Steve handcuffed Garth to the porch railing, called a patrol car to pick him up, and then hightailed it to the truck. "Come on, we've got to get Birdie." He called to Willow who was, as his mama would say, grinning like a 'possum eating a sweet potato.

Chapter 17

Willow and Steve circled Birdie's house. Nothing. No signs of life. Willow's phone rang. She ignored it. They had to find Birdie.

Steve looked through a window. The place was a disaster. He broke a window and declared, "probable cause." After crawling through the now open window he carefully checked all the rooms for Birdie or some clue as to what happened before opening the door for Willow.

Willow's phone rang again. This time she glanced at the number. It looked familiar to her but she couldn't place it. *Probably a salesman.* The phone beeped. The caller left a voice mail. She ignored it, again, then turned off the ringer.

Willow wandered the living room. She looked over the television. The dust on the back confirmed what she had figured all along, Garth didn't touch Birdie's television. She doubted he touched her stove either. As she walked closer to the couch, a vague scent captured her attention. It was familiar to her, but how? She bent down and gave the couch a good sniff. "Jordina!" She pulled out her phone, which had rang another three times since she had muted the thing, and listened to the voicemail.

"Steve!"

Steve came running. She replayed the voicemail on speaker.

"Willow, Birdie here. Meet me at the cabin. Alone. I have Jordina. We need to talk with you."

Steve spoke up. "You're not going there alone so don't even think it."

"I wouldn't dream of it. The woman's gone mad. I'm gonna need all the help I can get."

Twenty minutes later Willow pulled up in front of Clancy's cabin. Well, technically, Jordina's cabin now. She sat still for a few minutes wondering what was happening on the other side of the door and what she would find when she worked up the courage to go in. She steeled herself. She knew Steve was lurking in the woods nearby. He would get closer as soon as she was in the cabin and distracting Birdie from her normal jumpy self. She needed a chill pill, maybe some of those drugs they give kids these days to keep them sitting still at their desks.

She opened her car door and slowly walked toward the cabin, watching for movement from any of the street facing windows. Everything was still.

Willow raised her hand to knock and the door opened marginally, a hand reached out, grabbed her by the arm and pulled her in. Just as quickly the door closed behind her.

Willow's eyes took a moment to adjust to the darkness within the cabin. She looked around and heavy drapes were pulled over the windows. No wonder she couldn't see any movement. Sitting in a chair in the middle of the room was Jordina. She was tied at the feet and the hands. Her mouth was stuffed with what looked like a sock and her eyes were the complete description of fear. She grunted, trying to talk but nothing coming out was intelligible. Willow wanted to remove the sock but thought better of it. She followed Jordina's eyes which were looking toward Willow's right.

Birdie stood in the shadows with her handgun pointed at Willow. She decided to appeal to her southern practicalities. "Birdie, is that any way to treat a guest? You call me to your father's home then point a gun at me?"

"I didn't invite you as a guest, I invited you as a witness. Once Jordina signs her new will, you can leave." She knew Willow had her concealed carry. "Put your gun and your phone on the table."

Willow did as she was told. She hoped Birdie didn't go for a pat down. She had a backup gun in the waistband of her pants and a burner phone in her pocket. Steve was listening to every word.

"Once Jordina signs over the cabin to you, you can let us both go. She would want Clancy's daughter to have what is rightfully due her."

Jordina's eyes widened in surprise.

Birdie chirped out, "What do you mean by that?"

"You're his daughter, right?"

"When did you know?"

"I didn't know you were his daughter until today."

"But you knew I killed him. How?"

"It was a bunch of little things that started coming together. The day of the murder, you pulled up next to my truck and carried in the jugs of ice tea. And yet, later on when we were eating, you said you tried a new macaroni and cheese recipe, the one with olives. At first, I didn't put two and two together, but later, I remembered you walked away then came back and got the tea. You didn't have a crock pot in your hands. You had to have carried it in earlier, which would have put you at the range at the time of the murder. Bringing your dish to pass early was a good cover for being there, but not a very good way to cover your tracks if anyone had seen you."

She nodded. "That wasn't enough to convict me."

"No, and I might not have thought twice about it until I was here, looking through Clancy's scrapbook. I noticed a picture of a woman who looked nearly identical to you. A few days later when we came back, after the funeral, the picture was missing. Steve noticed Garth arrived late and made eye contact giving you the heads up. He'd found the picture. But neither of you knew he had copies tucked away in his closet. We searched through boxes and found a copy of the very same picture. But we also found other pictures, one of your mama holding a baby, a baby girl— you. After I saw the picture of your mama holding the fried chicken, it dawned on me what happened."

She stifled her tears. "I was looking for my mama's recipe. That's the most important thing to me. I didn't realize Clancy had a picture of my mom until Jordina told me there was a picture of me in his scrapbook, or at least someone who looked a lot like me. If I had known on the day of the funeral, I would have grabbed that too, then you would never have seen it."

"You looked for and found the recipe, which I'm guessing was your mama's famous recipe, since she won first place in the Southern Fried Chicken Cook-Off back before you were born. You wanted what was rightfully yours, or should have been yours had your mama have lived. You wanted that trophy for your mantle. You wanted it next to the other trophies you have on display there. Is that why you killed him?"

"The day you were at my house, the recipe was on the counter. I hid it. Clancy took credit for my mama's chicken. It made me angry. Not enough to kill him. I thought about it, but I didn't want to spend the rest of my life in a jail cell."

"Then why did you do it?"

She swallowed hard. "I kind of figured he was my dad. It made sense. He was a liar and a cheat. He stole a hero's reward from Jordina's grandpa, he stole my mother's chicken recipe. Heaven only knows what else he had done in his lifetime. He never said a word to me about my mother. He pretended he didn't recognize me— even though I'm identical to my mother. Who does that? I just wanted him to admit he was my father. So, one night, I invited myself out to the cabin and brought a bottle of Jack Daniels and I got him good and drunk. When I asked him about my mother he said he knew I was her daughter the first time he laid eyes on me. Then he admitted he was my dad. I was thrilled. I knew my mom had died under some suspicious circumstances but I guess I couldn't imagine my father would have anything to do with it. I thought we'd be a family. Don't get me wrong, I love my adoptive parents. They gave me a good life. They told me who my mom had been and that I still had some family in the area, mainly my uncle Garth. But, I wanted to know my parents."

She moved the curtain slightly and looked out the window. Not seeing anything, she continued. "Every adopted child wonders what was wrong with them. Aren't they loveable? Why weren't they wanted? I was no different. I majored in history in college and traced back my mother's life. I went through everything I could find. That's how I found Clancy. When I found out he was my father, I was willing to forgive everything. I didn't care that he wasn't reputable, that his character was often the subject of condemning whispers. Then he uttered something I'll never forget. He laughed and said I should have seen my mother's face the day he killed her. He killed my mother. The only reason he didn't kill me is I was with a babysitter." She started crying. "My father killed my mother." She pulled the picture out of her pocket and stared at it. "She was beautiful. She was happy."

Birdie looked at Willow with her big, blue, sorrowful eyes and that out-of-date pixie cut that mirrored her mother's. "I left, in fact, I ran. I drove home and sobbed. The next day when I had dried the tears and found my resolve, I decided to kill him. I wanted to see his face as he died, just like he watched my mother as he drained the life from her. I wanted him to think of her when he was gasping for breath. I wanted him to see my mother when he looked at me." She gasped for breath. "I talked Garth into helping me with the electrical work in the back yard. Clancy was the only one who ever went back there to smoke. I knew his schedule. I had watched him. Garth had taken care of the wires the night before the potluck, then he drove out and hid in the woods. He was careful to cut through the woods so he wasn't caught on camera. I knew the angles of all the video surveillance. I made sure he did too. Garth called me as soon as Clancy stepped out back for his nicotine fix. I was ready to confront him. I wasn't even certain he'd remember what he told me, he was so drunk."

She tucked the picture away, back in her pocket. "He had just lit up when I got the phone call. I hugged the building wall so I wouldn't be seen by the parking lot camera then stepped around the corner. He'd remembered just fine.

You know what he said to me? 'You really are the picture of your mama. Man, when you first showed up I thought you was a ghost coming back to haunt me. Then come to find out you're the product of me and your mama's little fling. I didn't figure I'd ever lay eyes on you again.' He laughed then he said, 'You should really go back to where you came from. There ain't nothin' for you here. Not unless you want to end up like your mama.'"

She was quiet. Willow wanted to keep her talking. "Is that when you killed him?"

Birdie jumped. She'd been in her own little world of hurt and heartache. "Most of the live wire was buried. Just the end was sticking up through the weeds. One good push and he stepped right back on it. Those cowboy boots he loved were perfect. I had to research those to make sure they would do the trick. All he had to do was step back and that metal bar in the heel caused him to light up like a Christmas tree. I stared at him and grinned. I did it. He would never hurt anyone again. Ever."

Birdie turned toward Jordina. "Now, I'll have his fortune and that is the best part of him. The best is yet to come."

Willow watched as Birdie undid Jordina's hands.

"Why don't you untie her legs too? She never did anything to you."

Birdie nearly screamed. "She stole my inheritance!"

Willow tried to calm her down. "Birdie, she didn't know you existed. And she didn't know that Clancy was leaving her anything. This isn't her fault. You already got the guy who hurt you— who hurt your mama."

Birdie paused for a few seconds, thinking. "If she doesn't die then what point is signing the will?"

Willow's heart sank.

Birdie stood behind Jordina who was openly crying, then handed her a pen and a clipboard. "This is your destiny. Now sign the will."

Jordina dropped the pen, not in rebellion but because her hands were shaking so terribly. Birdie slapped her.

Willow started to intervene but Birdie stepped back and pointed the gun at Willow. "Don't do it. You have no part of this. I have no reason to kill you but I will." Willow stepped back and put up her hands in submission. She noticed Steve who had come in through the back door. She didn't look his way again. She didn't want to give his presence up.

As Birdie bent down and picked up the pen, Steve crossed the room in three strides and knocked her to the ground. She struggled with him for control of the gun and there was a loud bang in the small confines of the cabin. Everyone was still, wondering who, if anyone, was hit.

Willow looked up from her ground position. Blood was pooling on the wood floor under Birdie. She yelled out, "Steve!" then ran to the tangled duo.

Steve lifted his head then rolled off the dead woman. He lay there, without moving, stunned at the events that just took place.

Willow ran to his side. "Are you OK? Are you hurt?"

He nodded then pointed to Jordina. Willow quickly removed the sock from her mouth. She was screaming so Willow held her close. "Stop. You're all right, everything's OK now. ."

They could hear sirens. Steve had called in back up before coming in the cabin. He was sure to hear about sending Willow in the cabin. Unfortunately, his superiors didn't know Willow. As if he had a choice.

The medical examiner removed Birdie's body for autopsy. Jordina was huddled in a corner talking with a detective. Steve was still covered in Birdie's blood and remained silent as he waited to leave. He'd already explained what happened.

Willow just wanted to get her man home and cleaned up. *Her man? Where did that come from?* She squeezed his hand. She heard a commotion at the door then saw Jordina stand up and start crying all over again. Jason ran to her. Willow watched them huddle together, he had his arms protectively around her. A few minutes later, the officer allowed her to leave.

Jordina stepped up to Willow. "Thank you." She looked to Steve. "Thank you both. Without you I'd be dead. I'm certain of it. You saved my life." She paused. "And thank you for saving my grandfather.

He nodded. "I'm glad you're OK. And as for your grandfather, you can thank Willow. She's the one who insisted he was innocent."

Jordina did as he instructed then told them both goodbye. Jason helped her through the door.

Steve stoked Willow's cheek. "You did good, real good. But I've never been so scared in my life. The thought of something happening to you." He broke down in tears. Willow wrapped her arms around him and just held him.

[130]

Chapter 18

Willow watched the bride as she walked down the aisle. Jordina was stunning, absolutely beautiful. She and Jason had decided they didn't want to wait. Life was too short and they wanted to make the most of all the time they had left.

Steve rested his hand on her knee then leaned over and whispered, "Before you know it, this will be Embry."

"Don't I know it? So much to do!" She shushed him. Willow looked around the church. It was filled. The fact surprised Willow. Usually a spur of the moment wedding wouldn't fill up a church. This one sure did. Of course, many of the attendees were Abel's buddies, all in uniform too. So many uniformed men and women were seated all throughout the church. Both old and young due to Abel's past service and Jason being in the Air Force. "We have so much to do but I guess it'll work out. Look at how well this one turned out and on such short notice."

An older lady turned around and gave her a stern warning look.

"Sorry," Willow whispered. She felt like she was in the library all over again. That was twice in the course of a couple of weeks she was told to be quiet.

Willow studied the bride as the pastor performed the ceremony. Her dress perfectly contrasted with her glistening mocha skin. Her make-up was flawlessly applied and she was just the perfect height to kiss her husband when they were pronounced man and wife. Willow had the order of the service memorized. Perhaps someday, she would be the leading lady. She looked at Steve and smiled.

Just when the kiss was supposed to happen, Jason and Jordina turned to the guests. "We have a very special surprise for you today." Jason passed the microphone to his bride.

"Most of you know my grandfather, Abel White. His strong arm escorted me down the aisle today. My grandfather has always been a hero to me. Today, the world is going to recognize him for the hero he truly is." She glanced at her grandfather who was sitting on the front row. "Grandpa, would you join us up here on the platform, please?"

He adamantly shook his head.

"Grandpa, we need you up here. Please come." The entire church started clapping.

He hesitantly stood up and looked around. He wasn't used to being in the limelight or being recognized for anything and his face showed it. He joined his granddaughter and new son-in-law on the platform, looking extremely uncomfortable.

The pastor walked off the platform and an elderly man in uniform walked on the stage. Every singled man and woman in uniform immediately stood at attention with a salute at the sight of him. "At ease." Then he added. "Please, be seated."

Everyone sat down and waited. From her seat, she couldn't see Abel's face, but she did watch as Jordina's maid of honor handed him a tissue.

The man who gained the platform began speaking. "We are here today to address a grave injustice. During the course of war, many errors are made. Grievous errors. This isn't the first and it certainly won't be the last. I'm not here to correct the error, because that happens to be the president's job. I'm simply here to extend an invitation to Abel White to Washington D.C. to receive the Medal of Honor for his exemplary service in the United States Army. His bravery and action on the battlefield go above and beyond any call of duty. His actions on that day saved the lives of 12 of his fellow servicemen. We are here to honor you today." He saluted Abel White who promptly saluted back. Once again, the whole place was on their feet. All the service men and women saluted, all the civilians clapped. Once the church was quiet again, Abel returned to his seat, as did his commanding officer.

The pastor returned to the platform. "This very well may be the best wedding I have ever been asked to officiate. It's not every day you get to meet a true hero. Jason and Jordina wanted to start their life together honoring the man who raised her as his own, oftentimes denying himself in the process. They wanted to start their lives out right." He smiled at Abel. "And I believe they have done just that." He looked out at the guests. "Now, for the moment you all have been waiting for. Jason, you may now kiss your bride."

Chapter 19

Willow loved the fair at night. All the lights dancing across the sky, the sounds of children laughing, and the sight of lovers walking hand in hand, all of it brought a smile to her lips. This time was special. It wasn't like the nights spent at the fair as a child, wonderment and awe in her eyes for the lights and prizes. Tonight she was enchanted for another reason. She looked at the man walking next to her. "Thanks for taking me to the fair." She hugged her stuffed animal to her chest, smiling with her eyes closed. "And thank you for winning me this bear." The slightly rugged brown bear was something she was going to proudly display in her house, leaned up against her decorative couch pillows. *I'm going to have to talk to Clover about this bear!*

"You are welcome. I can't imagine being anywhere else… or being with anyone else."

Her heart leapt in her chest at his words. It was something she loved about him, his directness.

"Besides, do you really think I'd miss out on funnel cake?" He stepped up to a vendor booth and bought one of the sweet treats, as he remembered her romantic description of her date at the fair.

Willow watched Steve as he waited for the funnel cakes. He was dressed simply: dark jeans, a T-shirt, and work boots. She gazed at him as if he was the most handsome man she'd ever seen. She playfully swatted at him as he returned with the sweet treat. "All right, Mister, why do you think I invited you? It's kind of creepy seeing a 44 year old woman alone at the fair just so she can eat funnel cake." Unable to resist the temptation any longer, she winked at him then took a bite. "Delicious." Once again, Willows eyes closed as she savored the sweet dessert in her mouth, the dough nearly melting upon contact.

Her eyes opened slowly as Steve bent down and kissed the powdered sugar off her lips. "Mmm, you taste as good as the funnel cake." She smiled.

They saved the Ferris wheel until last. The line had dwindled down as the night drew darker. Love struck teenagers giggled in front of them. Willow could still make out the blush on the girls' cheeks, even in the darkness. Finally it was their turn to get on the ride. Steve and Willow had a car to themselves, not that Willow would have stood for sharing with anyone. He draped his arm around her as they slowly made their way to the top, the car stopping every minute or so to allow someone off, then to re-load. Willow felt like those blushing teenagers in line. *How long has it been since I've felt like this?*

Steve interrupted her introspection. "I think this might be the most alone you and I have ever been… here at the top of the world. Or at least close."

That didn't help her nerves at all. Her hands clammed up a little. It had been a long time since she'd felt this way about any man. Willow was not one to be scared off by fear. She leaned into him, settled in, and stared at the dark sky. "It's beautiful. This is beautiful." She pointed out the constellations, at least the easy ones she'd known since childhood. "There's the big dipper and little dipper."

Steve reached up and laid his hand over hers in the air, guiding her hand to other constellations, ones she wasn't so familiar with. "Living in the country has its advantages. Much easier to see without the city lights getting in the way. I used to spend my nights as a young boy staring at the stars with my father. He taught me different constellations. I've never forgotten them. Some things just stick with you, ya know?" Steve

[137]

lowered his hand, guiding hers down with his, and laced their fingers together.

A couple of minutes passed and the giant wheel started turning. The two of them sat silently, watching the city, the sky, simply content in one another's company. As the cart started to descend, Steve gripped her hand a little tighter, not wanting to lose the moment where all that existed was one another.

He brought his free hand to her face, turning her face up into his so he could place a gentle kiss on her lips.

Willow's Broccoli Salad

- 1 bunch of broccoli, tops only chopped (4 cups)
- 1 bunch of green onions, chopped
- 3 oz slivered almonds, toasted
- 2 cups red grapes, halved
- 1/2 lb bacon, crumbled
- 8 oz grated cheddar cheese

Dressing:

- 1 cup mayonnaise (not salad dressing)
- 1/3 cup sugar
- 1/2 cup grated Parmesan cheese

Combine broccoli, green onions, and grapes. Top with dressing and refrigerate overnight. Right before serving add almonds, bacon, and cheddar cheese.

Willow's Chicken Pot Pie

Simple ingredients, yet delicious.

- 2 premade pie crusts brought to room temperature (or use your favorite recipe)
- 4 chicken breasts, cubed
- 1 onion, chopped
- 1 can cream of chicken soup
- 8 oz shredded or cubed Velveeta
- 16 ouz frozen mixed vegetables
- 4 oz 2% milk

Sauté chicken and onion in two tablespoons grapeseed oil or olive oil on medium heat. Add soup, Velveeta, milk, and frozen vegetables. Cook for five minutes, or until just starting to bubble.

Line 2 quart round glass casserole dish with pie crust. Let the crust hang over the sides. Fill with hot chicken filling. Place second pie crust over the filling. Fold the two crusts together, crimping with your thumbs until all the overhanging crust is incorporated into the top crust. Cut four lines in top crust to vent.

Bake at 350 degrees for 35-40 minutes or until crust is lightly browned.

Note: The women prefer the broccoli, cauliflower, carrot mix in my family while the men prefer the corn, green beans, peas, and carrot mix. Both are delicious.

Willow's Sausage Gravy

The key to delicious sausage gravy is bacon.

- 1/2- 1 lb bacon
- 1 lb breakfast sausage
- Sprinkle of flour
- Milk for desired consistency

Fry bacon in large fry pan or electric skillet. Remove bacon and set aside. Add a good bulk sausage to the bacon grease. Fry until cooked thoroughly. Remove sausage from pan and set aside. Turn pan to medium heat and sprinkle flour in pan until mixed with grease in a nice roux. Let the roux bubble for 3-4 minutes so flour flavor is cooked out of mixture. Slowly add milk, stirring constantly, until gravy is desired thickness. Some like a really thick gravy, some like a thinner gravy. Adjust how much milk you add accordingly. Once the desired thickness is reached, turn off and add sausage to the gravy.

Best tasting gravy, ever.

Steve's French Dip

- 4 lbs chuck roast
- 1 can beef consume
- 2 cans French onion soup
- 1/3 cup soy sauce
- 1 tbs minced garlic
- 1 tbs minced onion
- 3 tbs browning sauce
- 1 cup water
- 2 beef bouillon cubes

Combine ingredients in crock pot. Cook on low for 8 hours or until roast is fork tender. Remove roast and fork apart, removing fat as you go.

Transfer liquid to a medium size saucepan. Reduce to about half. Serve with toasted hoagie buns and slices of both provolone and mozzarella cheese.

Willow's Chocolate Chip Cookies

- 1 cup butter, softened
- 1/4 cup sugar
- 3/4 cup brown sugar, firmly packed
- 1-3 oz package of vanilla instant pudding mix
- 2 large eggs
- 1 tsp vanilla
- 1 tsp baking soda
- 2 1/4 cups flour
- 12 oz chocolate chips

Combine butter, sugars, vanilla, and pudding mix in large mixing bowl. Beat until smooth. Add eggs. Beat until mixed in. Sprinkle baking soda over mix and beat in. Add flour gradually, beating while you do so. Stir in chocolate chips. Drop by teaspoonful onto ungreased baking sheet. Slightly flatten. Bake at 375 degrees for 8-10 minutes.

Willow's Fried Chicken

- Fryer chicken, quartered or halved

Marinade:

Mix marinade ingredients and marinate chicken no more than 3 hours.

- Juice of two lemons
- Equal part sparkling dry white wine
- 1 tsp salt
- 1 tsp pepper
- ¼ tsp cloves
- 2 bay leaves
- ½ cup chopped green onions

Batter:

- 1 ½ cup flour
- Cold sparkling dry white wine
- 3 egg yolks
- 1 tsp salt

Mix flour and enough wine to make a pancake like batter consistency. Add 3 egg yolks and salt. Dip chicken into batter and fry in 350 degree oil until done.

When chicken is finished, place on a cooling rack.

Fry completely dry parsley and use to garnish (very important).

This is an Old English Recipe handed down through the generations.

Please enjoy this excerpt from 'Bobbing for One Bad Apple', Book 5 of the Willow Crier Cozy Mystery Series

Willow walked in a slow circle. Everything in her ice cream shop had taken on the appearance of fall. Various shades of red, yellow, orange, and brown were scattered everywhere. Turtle's(Tuttle?) fall festival was celebrated in conjunction with Halloween, and Willow wanted to be sure her store was decorated to the hilt. If she couldn't have the real thing—fall in the north where fall really happened—she'd improvise. She had trees with fall leaves, pumpkins, gourds, bales of hay, even a scarecrow. She wanted to have bobbing for apples but Molly talked her into have a maze in the small open lot behind the ice cream store as her attraction, and thereby giving Molly the Apple Bobbing attraction.

She was looking forward to the celebration. In a few hours children dressed as ghosts and goblins would be visiting her shop for complimentary apple donuts and spiced apple cider. Of course, she would have other apple and pumpkin goodies for sale too, like her German Apple cake and her grandmother's apple pie, as well as scrumptious pumpkin bars. A personal favorite. Her mouth watered just thinking about her favorite fall treats.

The door opened and Willow's face fell. The jogging complainers, as she liked to call them, came calling. She stood behind the counter and waited for the barrage of instructions. As well as the complaints.

He, being the gentleman that he was, ordered first. "I'll have a low fat milk latte, 2 shots of espresso, no foam, extra hot, with three packets of Splenda stirred in well." No hello. No please. No thank you.

Willow looked to his wife, at least she thought she was his wife. "I'm lactose intolerant, so I'll have the same except make mine with soy milk, oh, and Splenda seems to upset my tummy so use Agave Nectar."

Willow tried very hard not to roll her eyes. "We still do not have Agave Nectar. I'm sorry." She gave her the same story the day before. She told her when she made a run to the city she'd swing by Whole Foods, until then, she'd have to use one of the sweeteners she had on hand.

"Uh, sheesh, I miss home. You can't get a decent cup of coffee in this town." She told her husband was looking at his watch for the tenth time. "Fine. Use Splenda. I'll suffer."

"You could use sugar." Willow replied.

The gasp coming from both joggers was loud enough to be heard in the far corner of the ice cream side of her shop.

"Sugar? You must be joking. Haven't touched the stuff in years. It's poison." Her face pinched, as if she were in pain, when she glanced at the treats behind the glass counter. "You really shouldn't sell that stuff. Doing so is irresponsible and advocating bad eating habits."

"Karla, don't distract her. You know these people can barely do one thing at a time, let alone multitask." He smiled a tight smile in Willow's direction then he lowered his voice. "She'll probably mess the coffee up as it is."

Karla laughed. "Good one Flynn."

Willow mimicked their New York accent to a "T" as she turned around to grab the soy milk. "Did you hear that Janie? Can't get a decent cup of cawhfee in dis town."

Janie was making shakes for a group of teenage girls. "Shh, they'll hear you."

"I don't give a rip. Rude, arrogant, stuck up…"

Janie placed her hand over Willow's mouth. "Be nice. Don't lower yourself to their level. We've

[149]

got to keep our spirits up. The kids will be coming soon."

Willow licked the chocolate that had transferred from Janie's hand. "Mm, that's good. I might have to have one of those later."

Willow made their drinks with an attitude, not that they noticed. She doubted they considered anyone besides themselves. She handed them their drinks, collected the money, and sent them on their way. The sooner she had them out of her hair, the sooner she could manage an attitude adjustment and finish prepping for the kids. She glanced at her watch.

"Janie, I'm going to go check and see how Embry and Marshall are doing on the maze then I'm going to walk to the café and see how Molly is doing. I'll be back in a bit."

Everyone was hands on, including the part-timers, for the event so she wasn't concerned about leaving Janie shorthanded. The maze was awesome. Embry and Marshall each had a chair, one at the beginning and one at the end of the maze and Walkie Talkies to keep in touch. How many in, how many out. Marshall was sitting at the exit with the big bowl of candy. He said he'd sacrifice himself. Embry had the entry. No candy for her. She was trying to lose weight before the wedding.

Willow meandered down to the café where Molly had made a giant batch of caramel to go with the apples the kids were bobbing for. A little something sweet to dip the apples in. It was a holiday, after all.

She made a sound of disgust as she walked through the front door to see Flynn and Karla arguing with poor Molly. She heard Molly's reply to whatever they had been complaining about.

"This isn't New York or California. This is Oklahoma. We do things a bit different. At this time of year we actually give our kids candy." She gave Karla a look that Willow had a hard time interpreting.

Karla stuck her nose up in the air and walked out. Flynn was right behind her.

Willow held the door open for them as they flew by her without so much as a thank you. She wiped her hands together, as if there was garbage on them she had to get it off. "I see you've tossed the rubbish."

"If only. He thinks the Sun comes up just to hear him crow. And she's no better. You can take the girl out of the country but you can't take the country out of the girl."

Willow stared, dumbfounded. "What on Earth are you talking about, Molly?"

"Ain't it obvious? The man thinks he's the authority on all things. He won't shut up."

"No, I got that. I'm talking about Karla. What did you mean?"

"Oh, I forget you're not from around these parts. Karla's about as southern as a girl can get. She was born and raised an Okie. Then off she went up north to college and she decided we're not sophisticated enough for her, so she migrated. Claims she was born in the wrong skin."

"You have to be kidding me?"

"Nope. Her daddy and mama live on the ranch next to mine. You'd never know it but growing up that girl was at my house more than she was her own." Molly shook her head. "My niece has broken my sister's heart."

Willow's mouth dropped. Niece? She swallowed hard and remained silent.

Molly continued. "This is the first time she's been home since she left for college. Hardly ever calls her mama. Missy's learned the hard way she's got to trust God with Karla. Otherwise she'd be a worryin' mess."

Willow headed back to her own shop. She waved to Steve and his deputy who were letting kids sit in the front seat of the police car and passing out candy. All evening, in between the princesses and knights, Willow thought about the rude couple from New York. How could that girl be an Okie? Since moving from Wisconsin, she complained about the heat, the bugs, the snakes, her allergies, and the tornadoes. But never the people. The friendliest people on earth. She'd swear by it. What in the world happened to that girl?

The next morning, Willow woke to the sound of her chirping cell phone. "Darn. Why didn't I turn off the ringer?" She picked it up and muttered, "This better be good."

Janie responded. "Get down to Molly's, now. Flynn went bobbing for apples and he never came up."

Please enjoy this excerpt from 'In-Laws and Out-Laws', Book 1 of the Brother Bay Cozy Mystery Series

Millie MacDonald collapsed, exhausted, onto her and Mac's king size bed. In fact, they both rested their heads against the fluffy down pillows at exactly the same moment.

The amount of work that goes into opening a bed and breakfast is insane. They'd been open a month but had bought the place over a year ago. Updating the old inn had been a lengthy process. Brother's Bay, right next to the iconic Sister's Bay in Door County, was the perfect location for finally realizing her dream. Besides, while the summer months were crazy busy, the winter months moved along at a snail's pace. Mac could sit by the fire and write that novel he'd always talked about and they could travel and see the world, another one of their dreams, beginning with Ireland.

She sighed and before she could attempt to get comfortable, her husband started snoring. How does he do that? Does his brain go on strike?

Doesn't he think? About anything! What started as a soft, barely there sleeping wheeze, within seconds transgressed into a loud, obnoxious ground shaking snore. *Great, I'll never get to sleep now.*

Millie gave her husband a light kick then quickly closed her eyes, hoping he would think he woke himself with his snoring. She lied perfectly still, waiting. He was silent for about two seconds before a loud snort erupted from his side of the bed. "Ugh!" She yelled into her pillow. Might as well get back up.

She slipped her feet into her pink fuzzy slippers, her daughter's idea, not hers, and started for their private living quarters. She paused next to her husband and watched his chest rise and fall with each breath. Who was she kidding? She'd give up a kidney to sleep like him. Okay, maybe not a kidney. But definitely the spare tire around her midriff. She shook her head and quietly slipped out of their bedroom.

Millie loved the small part of the house she and Mac inhabited. The top floor of the white Victorian mansion was all theirs. Their master suite was luxurious. Perhaps not as much as the suites below, but certainly lovely. Besides the master, there was a small guest room, an office, sitting area, and an eat-in kitchen. Certainly enough room for the two of them.

The two floors below consisted of five guest suites, a library, a large kitchen, a sitting room, and a dining room. A small office off the kitchen served as command central for the employees she and Mac used to help make the B&B run as efficiently as possible.

The moans and creaks of the old house gave it character. She dismissed the local legend that the place was haunted. Ridiculous. Just because someone died in a residence didn't mean it was haunted. Besides, the old woman had died of natural causes. Or so the story went. Of course, it was also common knowledge that today's crime scene investigators would be able to run tests that weren't available back then. If someone got away with murder there was nothing to be done for it now. Gossips—always speculating.

At the moment, all five guest suites were filled and would be for the next three days. Which meant her in-laws last minute decision to visit put them in her and Mac's small guest bedroom. They were to arrive the next day. No wonder she couldn't sleep.

She put the tea kettle on and gathered up some loose leaf chamomile. Perhaps that will help. Her newfangled electric tea pot turned off and she poured the boiling water over her tea ball then inhaled deeply of the fragrant tea. She added a touch of honey then blew the hot liquid for a few seconds before taking a sip. "Mm…this is good."

She heard the bed groan under the weight of her husband as he turned. She leaned back and closed her eyes.

Millie woke with a start and looked around, confused. The sun was already peeking through the blanket of darkness. She jumped and startled the still nearly full cup of tea she'd made the night before. "Goodness. I'm going to be late with breakfast." She mumbled as she rubbed her sore neck.

Regardless of running a little late, she took an extra few minutes under the hot shower, hoping that would loosen her neck up. The smell of coffee assaulted her nostrils. "Thank you, Mac." She said out loud as she lathered up. A cup would be waiting for her when she descended the top floor.

She dressed in a late summer outfit, one that still offered her a reasonable amount of air flow. She hated to wear sleeveless shirts, her arms certainly weren't sculptured, but the least she could reasonably get away with wearing, the better. Especially when the summer sun was still causing the black top to radiate heat waves.

She entered the kitchen at full speed.

Mac was at the table with a cup of coffee and the newspaper. "Woah. Slow down. Take time to smell the roses." He pushed her coffee toward her place at the kitchen table.

"Mac, I don't have time to smell the roses. Besides, there aren't any." She turned the oven on then turned back to him. "Okay, remind me again why we opened this business. We both hate mornings. Are we gluttons for punishment or what?" She took a big swig of coffee then put her hands on her hips. "Why didn't you wake me up?"

She removed the breakfast casserole and the muffin mix from the refrigerator as she waited for his answer.

"I thought you could use the extra rest. I noticed you went missing after lights out."

"Couldn't sleep, again. Any other time I'd kiss you. But, your parents are due right after breakfast and we have a full house. You should have woke me." She chastised as she checked off items on her mental checklist.

The breakfast sideboard had already been set the night before with Millie's china coffee cups, juice glasses, linen napkins, silverware, plates, and butter.

"Mac, can you get the jams out of the fridge and put them in their serving dishes?" She loved her big commercial stove. She popped the casserole in one side and the muffins in the other side. She poured coffee, orange juice, and water in their proper containers and carried them to the dining room. She glanced at the time. Forty five minutes until breakfast.

Mac filled her antique dishes with homemade blackberry, cherry almond, and cherry apple jams. He also placed a dish of apple butter on the buffet. "Where's Lucy?"

Millie shook her head. "I don't know. She didn't call to say she'd be late. I'll chat with her after breakfast, if she shows up that is."

Lucy was their kitchen help. She was at least 10 years older than Millie, if not more, but no one dared ask. She was a feisty little spitfire who had more energy than some teenagers Millie had come across. Sometimes she was downright rude. Usually, she was reliable. And she was a local in need of a job. Social security wasn't cutting it. Millie's forehead creased with worry. In the past month she'd come to rely on the old biddy. Not only for kitchen help but the woman knew everything about everyone in their small bay town. She gave Millie the scoop on the inn. Every last sordid detail. Even speculated that the old woman who had died some hundred years before did not die of natural causes, but was murdered. She said the proof was in this house—somewhere. That's why the place was supposedly haunted. Not that Millie believed a word of it.

The back door creaked open. Lucy made her grand entrance. "Sorry I'm late. My cat went missing. Darn thing. Makes a run for the door every time it opens. I think she thinks she's being held against her will." She thought about it then added, "I guess she's right." She piled her long grey hair on top her head and secured it with a couple of big pins. "I would have called but I thought the time would be better spent finding the cat. "What else needs doing?"

Millie opened the oven to check the muffins. "You can start slicing the fruit."

Lucy washed her hands then jumped in and got right to work. "You remember what tomorrow is?"

Mac responded, "I sure do."

Millie looked at her husband and mumbled, "Since when do you follow the local gossip?"

He was obviously proud to know something she didn't. "According to Lucy, it's not gossip. It's local legend. 100 years ago, right after this house was built, Miss Mary Hettiger, a direct descendent of Increase and Mary Clafflin, the first settlers of Door County, was found dead on her bed. She was dressed real pretty with a rose in her hand. Now, her death was ruled natural causes but everyone knew something fishy was going on. Who put the rose in her hand? Why was she lying on the bed like Snow White?" He leaned into his wife and raised his eyebrows. "She's the one who haunts the place."

Millie rolled her eyes. "Quit talking nonsense. You're just doing this to get her going and you know it."

Lucy piped up. "He knows truth when he hears it. You'll see. Somethin' bad's gonna happen. Mark my words."

Millie ignored both of them and finished getting breakfast on the buffet in the dining room. Everything was in its place when the first guests arrived. "Good morning. I hope you slept well."

The blushing bride vigorously nodded her head and smiled.

The newlyweds were in the bridal suite. She was surprised they didn't order breakfast to be served in their room. Most young couples did. Although they had been in residence for nearly a week. Perhaps they were ready to interact with other humans. "I'm so glad you two could join us this morning. Everything is ready. Just help yourselves. We do breakfast buffet style."

Millie watched Mac go into Irish mode. His voice deepened by a couple of degrees and that

Irish lilt would magically attach itself to each word spoken. Of course, it was even worse when he led guests into the sitting room and explained the MacDonald crest in the place of pride above the fireplace mantle. That would come later. She was sure of it.

The other guests should be here soon, Millie said to herself. She realized some of the bed and breakfasts delivered the morning meal each day to their guests. Millie wanted that old fashioned gathering to get to know her guests. Of course, if the guests insisted they wanted a private breakfast, then she acquiesced. But she encouraged them to join the breakfast gathering with the enticement of traditional Irish folk lore. Told in Irish brogue, naturally.

Todd and Susie, the newlyweds, were seated and already eating when Mrs. Hampton, a single woman visiting family in the area, gingerly picked up her plate and began to fill it.

"How are you this morning, Mrs. Hampton?"

"Just fine dear. Just fine. Breakfast looks lovely. I'm so glad I chose to stay here. Heaven knows what I'd be getting if I'd stayed with my relations." She topped her muffin with cherry apple jam then sat across from the newlyweds.

Lucy appeared with a tray. "The Galley Suite asked for breakfast to be delivered." She loaded up two plates with the various offerings and set off for the second floor.

Right after Lucy left with her delivery, Mr. Philips, the business man from Chicago, flitted into the dining room. "Have to hurry. You have anything I can just take with me? A to-go cup with coffee, maybe?"

"Oh, yes, I'll be right back." Millie filled a disposable coffee cup with the local brew and a covered dish with a couple of muffins and some fruit. "Perhaps you can eat when you get where you're going." She tucked some plastic silverware in the container as well as a napkin and handed them to the pacing man.

"Oh thank you. Perhaps tomorrow I'll be able to sit down and enjoy your wonderful breakfast. Sunday's my day off. I won't have anything to do but relax."

Mac spoke up in his best Irish accent. "And a good breakfast ye shall have."

Mr. Hampton startled slightly then realized it was part of the Irish charm the Inn was recognized for and relaxed. His attempt at an Irish reply came out between an English and an Australian accent, "Tomorrow, then." He laughed as he turned to leave.

Mr. Phillips exited the dining room and a couple of minutes later, Millie heard his car pull out in the morning traffic. She said to Mac, "That just leaves Mr. Normal." As host and hostess, they didn't sit down to eat until all their guests were fed. Millie could tell Mac was getting impatient. "I'll go check on him."

Just as she reached the second floor landing, she saw Mr. Normal exiting the Fish Suite. He looked up and when he saw her, he blushed.

"Mrs. MacDonald. I was on my way to breakfast when I remembered I'd left my wallet sitting on the nightstand. I accidently opened the wrong suite door. I was just going back to mine now. I'll be right down."

"No problem, Mr. Normal. I'll see you in a few minutes. I tried to call but didn't get an answer. I just thought I'd check to see if you were all right. I thought perhaps you'd changed your mind about breakfast."

He stuttered. "And miss one of your breakfasts? I think not." He opened his own suite door and disappeared for a few seconds before joining her on the staircase.

Millie made a mental note to make a little breakfast intention card for her guests to fill out. That would take the second guessing out of the equation.

After Mr. Normal filled his plate, Mac jumped in and loaded his own plate. By the time all this took place, the newlyweds bid everyone goodbye for the day. They were off on a lighthouse tour followed by a trip to Washington Island. Tomorrow they would be leaving their little love nest and getting back to the real world.

Millie finally sat down next to her husband to enjoy her breakfast. At least Mr. Normal and Mrs. Hampton were still seated and enjoying a leisurely breakfast. "So, what do you two have planned for the day?"

Mrs. Hampton swallowed a bite then answered, "I'm spending the day with my sister and her family. I'm sure I'll come back with a pounding headache. Those grandchildren of hers are hellions. They listen to nothing and do nothing but scream all day. The only part of the vacation that is lovely is staying at this inn. I can't imagine what my head would feel like if I'd accepted the invitation to stay with them. I shudder at the thought." A horn honked outside the Inn. "Oh that must be them." She shook her head. "It used to be rude to sit in your car and honk your horn to get someone's attention. When did people get so lazy they can't come knock on a door anymore?" She stood up. "Thank you for breakfast. It was delicious." She started to walk away then turned.

"Oh, and I almost forgot. The rose in my room is lovely. Thank you."

Millie tilted her head as she watched Mrs. Hampton leave. Mr. Normal never answered Millie's question and quickly excused himself. Once they were both gone Millie asked Mac, "Do you have any idea what she's talking about?"

"Nope. Not a clue. Someone must love her though." He stood up and refilled his plate as the front door jangled open.

Millie sunk down in her chair. She could smell the perfume from the dining room. Her mother-in-law had arrived.

A Yankee's Guide to Southern Phrases

Bless Your Heart: The most back handed kind words spoken in the south. Means, while you're sweet, you're also stupid, you don't quite get it and I feel sorry for you.

Fixin to: About to do something, almost ready, thinking about doing something.

Nervous as a long tail cat in a room full of rockin' chairs: Nervous to the point of being jumpy.

Reckon: So suppose or believe something is true.

Yankee: Anyone originating north of the Mason Dixon line.

Redneck: Polite, blue collar individual who loves hunting, country music, and blue jeans. Add alcohol and anything can happen.

Y'all: You guys

All y'all: More than five people

I could eat the north end of a south-bound polecat: Starving!

Lil' Dogie: A motherless calf, a calf separated from its cow.

Hankering: Craving something

Fair to middlin': Doing okay
Three sheets to the wind: Drunker than a skunk
Passel: A whole bunch
Hold your horses: Be patient
Grinning like a possum eating a sweet potato:
Happy as can be

Author Bio

Lilly York? (aka Darlene Shortridge, author of Contemporary Christian Fiction) How about Lilly Belle; a mis-plant northerner, living in a southern world. Southern charm is lost among late nights with a two year old granddaughter, heat flashes competing with hell, copious re-runs of Murder She Wrote with Jessica Fletcher catching the bad guy, and a vivid imagination keeping insanity at bay.

In both humor and mystery, Lilly draws inspiration from terrible twos, a 24 year old daughter who questions her sanity, a son who constantly spews bad puns, and a husband who has selective hearing. Though, that's perfectly alright with her, because what can you love more than a good laugh and a family so dysfunctional they almost seem functional?

To stay informed on the whereabouts and goings-on of the Willow Crier Cozy Mystery Characters as well as upcoming releases, recipes and maybe a clue or two, join Lilly's e-mail club by going to…

LillyYork.com